THE EMPEROR'S PEARL

It all began on the night of the Poo-yang dragonboat races, when the drummer of the favourite boat suddenly collapsed under the astonished eyes of the spectators on the banks of the Grand Canal. Then, at the start of his inquiry into this curious case, Judge Dee, the famous bearded detective of ancient China, finds the body of a beautiful young woman, cruelly murdered in a deserted country mansion.

He discovers that these two deaths are connected with an ancient tragedy, involving the theft of the Emperor's Pearl, a near-legendary treasure that was stolen from the Imperial Harem one hundred years before. And in the background of the investigation looms the terrifying figure of the White Lady, the River Goddess whose colossal marble statue stands lonely on the bloodstained altar of her ruined shrine. Protected by the impenetrable forests of the haunted Mandrake Grove, her sinister influence seems to permeate the whole complex situation.

Clues are few and elusive, but gradually the judge assembles all the pieces of the complicated jigsaw puzzle and, in one bold and brilliant move, uncovers the strange secret of *The Emperor's Pearl*.

Judge Dee Mysteries Available from
Chicago:

THE EMPEROR'S PEARL

A Judge Dee Mystery

by

ROBERT VAN GULIK

*With eight illustrations
drawn by the author in Chinese style*

THE UNIVERSITY OF CHICAGO PRESS

The University of Chicago Press, Chicago 60637

ISBN 0-226-84872-8 (pbk.)

Library of Congress Cataloging-in-Publication Data

Gulik, Robert Hans van, 1910–1967.
    The emperor's pearl : a Judge Dee mystery / by
    Robert van Gulik : with eight illustrations drawn by
    the author in Chinese style.
        p.   cm. — (Judge Dee mysteries)
    1. Dee Jen-Djieh (Fictitious character)—Fiction.
    2. Judges—China—Fiction. I. Title. II. Series:
    Gulik, Robert Hans van, 1910–1967.
    Judge Dee mystery.
    PR9130.9.G8E63   1994
    823'.914—dc20   93-50923
                                         CIP

⊗ The paper used in this publication meets the
minimum requirements of the American National
Standard for Information Sciences—Permanence of
Paper for Printed Library Materials, ANSI Z39.48-1992.

ILLUSTRATIONS

*There is a plan of Mr Kou's library on page 149, and
pages 6–7 show a picture of the dragonboat races.*

DRAMATIS PERSONAE

Note that in Chinese the surname—here printed in capitals—precedes the personal name

Main characters

DEE Jen-djieh — Magistrate of Poo-yang, a thriving district in Central China, on the Grand Canal

HOONG Liang — his trusted personal adviser, Sergeant of the tribunal

Persons connected with 'The Case of the Dead Drummer'

PIEN Kia — a doctor of medicine

TONG Mai
SIA Kwang — vagrant students of literature

Persons connected with 'The Case of the Murdered Slave-maid'

KOU Yuan-liang — a wealthy collector of curios

Mrs Kou, named Gold Lotus — his First Lady

The Amber Lady — his secondary wife, a former slave-girl

Persons connected with 'The Case of the Emperor's Pearl'

YANG — owner of a large antique shop

KWANG Min — a drug-dealer from the capital

Others

SHENG Pa — Head of the Beggars' Guild

Miss Violet LIANG — Owner of a training hall. Original Mongolian name Altan Tsetseg Khatun, 'Golden Flower Princess'

I

A tall man was lighting a stick of incense on the altar of the River Goddess.

After he had stuck it in the bronze burner, he looked up at the serene face of the life-size statue, lit by the uncertain light of the only oil-lamp that hung from the smoke-blackened rafters of the small shrine. The goddess seemed to smile, faintly.

'Yes, you may well be happy!' the man said bitterly. 'Over in your sacred grove, you took her away from me just when I was about to sprinkle you with her blood. But tonight I have chosen a new victim for you, duly prepared for sacrifice. This time I shall . . .'

He checked himself and cast an anxious glance at the old priest in a tattered brown robe, sitting on the bench at the entrance of the shrine. The priest looked out over the river-bank, gaily decorated with coloured lampions, then bent again over his prayer-book. He paid not the slightest attention to the lonely visitor.

The man looked up once more at the goddess.

The wood of the statue was left plain; the sculptor had cleverly used the grain for accentuating the folds of the robe that descended from her rounded shoulders. She was sitting cross-legged on a many-petalled lotus flower, her left hand resting in her lap, the other raised in a gesture of benediction.

'You are beautiful!' the man whispered hoarsely. Staring intently at the still face above him, he went on: 'Tell me, why must all beauty be evil? Tempting man, enticing him with coy smiles and sidelong glances, then to repel him?

Repel him with a contemptuous sneer, break him, then haunt him for ever afterwards . . .?' He clutched at the edge of the altar, a maniacal glint in his distended eyes. 'It is right they are punished,' he muttered angrily. 'It is right that the knife is plunged in their treacherous hearts when they lie, stretched out, naked on the altar before you, right that their . . .'

Suddenly he broke off, startled. He thought he had seen a frown crease the smooth forehead of the goddess, round the pearl gleaming in its centre. Then, with a sigh of relief, he wiped the perspiration from his face. It had been the shadow of a moth, flying past the oil-lamp.

He compressed his lips tightly, cast a dubious glance at the statue, and turned away. He stepped up to the old priest, engrossed in his mumbled prayers. He tapped his thin, bony shoulder.

'Can't you leave your goddess alone tonight, for once?' he asked with forced joviality. 'The dragonboat races will be starting soon. Look, they are lining up the boats already under the marble bridge!' Taking a handful of coppers from his sleeve, he resumed: 'Here, take these and have a good meal in the restaurant over there!'

The old man looked up at him with his tired, red-rimmed eyes. He did not take the coins.

'I can't leave her, sir. She is a vengeful one, she is.'

He bent his grey head again over his prayer-book.

Despite himself the man shivered. Uttering an obscene curse he brushed past the old priest and went down the flight of stone steps leading to the road along the river-bank. He would have to ride back to the city in a hurry, to be there in time for the finish of the boat race.

II

'That's the six I had been waiting for!' Judge Dee said with satisfaction to his First Lady. He added a domino to the complicated pattern that was forming on the square table.

His three wives made no comment; they were studying their hands. In the gathering dusk it was difficult to discern the red pips on the bamboo dominoes. The judge and his three ladies were sitting on the high platform in the stern of the official barge, moored somewhat apart from the other boats lying stem to stern along the bank of the Canal. It was the fifth day of the fifth moon, the day of the yearly Dragonboat Festival. Since early in the afternoon the citizens of Poo-yang had been streaming out of the south gate, towards the point on the Canal where the grandstand indicated that, later in the night, the dragonboats would finish the race. There their magistrate, Judge Dee, would hand out the prizes to the contending crews.

The magistrate was required only to perform that ceremony, but Judge Dee, always eager to take part in the feasts of the people entrusted to his care, had wanted to assist at the races from the beginning. Therefore he had already left the city one hour before sunset, together with his suite, carried in three palankeens. They had installed themselves on his large official barge, anchored opposite the grandstand, and there partaken of a simple dinner of rice and sweet soup, just like the several thousand citizens that were crowding the smaller craft lining both banks. After dinner they had settled down to a game of dominoes, waiting till the moon would be out and the boat races start. It was getting cooler now; sounds of singing and laughter came

11

over the water. The garlands of lampions that decorated all the boats and barges were being lit; the smooth black water reflected their gay colours.

It was a fairy-like scene, but the four people round the domino table, engrossed in the game, paid scant attention to it. Dominoes was the favourite game in Judge Dee's household, they played it very seriously, and in a complicated form. And now they were approaching the final, decisive phase.

The Third Lady selected a domino from those set up in front of her. As she added it to the pieces on the table, she said to the two maids who were squatting by the tea-stove:

'Better light our lampions too, I can hardly see what I am doing!'

'I pass!' Judge Dee announced. He looked up annoyed as the old house steward appeared on deck and came up to the table. 'What is it now again? Has that mysterious visitor come back?'

Half an hour before, when the judge and his ladies had interrupted their game and were standing at the railing to watch the scenery, a stranger had boarded the barge. But, when the steward was going to announce him, the man had said that, on second thought, he did not want to disturb the judge.

'No, Your Honour, it is Dr Pien and Mr Kou,' the greybeard said respectfully.

'Show them up!' Judge Dee said with a sigh. Pien Kia and Kou Yuan-liang were in charge of the organization of the dragonboat race. Judge Dee knew them only by sight, they did not belong to the small circle of notables of Pooyang whom he met regularly at official functions. Dr Pien was a well-known physician and owner of a large drug store, Mr Kou a wealthy art-collector. 'They won't be long!' he added, with a reassuring smile to his three wives.

12

JUDGE DEE RECEIVES MR KOU AND DR PIEN

'As long as you don't tamper with our dominoes!' the First Lady said, pouting. She and the two others turned their pieces face down, then they rose and withdrew behind the screen placed across the platform. For ladies are not allowed to meet men not connected with the household.

Judge Dee had risen also, he answered with a nod the low bows of the two solemn, tall gentlemen who had appeared on deck. They were dressed in long summer robes of thin white silk and wore black gauze caps on their heads.

'Sit down, gentlemen!' the judge said affably. 'I suppose you have come to report that all is set for the races?'

'Indeed, sir!' Dr Pien replied in his dry, precise voice. 'When Mr Kou and I left Marble Bridge just now, all nine boats had been lined up at the starting-point.'

'Did you get good crews?' Judge Dee asked, then snapped at the maid who was arranging the teacups on the table: 'Don't disturb those dominoes!'

While the judge quickly turned the pieces in the pool face down again, Dr Pien replied: 'There was even more enthusiasm than usual, sir. The twelve rowers for each boat were recruited in no time at all. There'll be a keen competition, for the crew of Number Two is composed entirely of boatmen from the Canal who are determined to beat the townspeople! Mr Kou and I saw to it that all the men were suitably entertained with food and wine in the restaurant of Marble Bridge Village. Now they are raring to go!'

'Your boat is the favourite, Dr Pien!' Kou Yuan-liang remarked wryly. 'Mine hasn't got a chance, it's too heavy!'

'But it'll provide the historical background, Mr Kou,' the judge told him. 'I heard that your boat is an exact replica of the dragonboats used by our ancestors.'

A pleased smile crossed Kou's handsome, vivacious face. He said: 'I take part in the races mainly to see to it that the old traditions are faithfully observed.'

14

Judge Dee nodded. He knew that Kou had devoted a life-time to antiquarian studies and was an ardent collector of curios. The judge reflected that he must ask Kou to show him his collection of paintings some day. He said:

'I am glad to hear that, Mr Kou. This feast has been celebrated on this date since times immemorial, everywhere in the Empire where there is a river, canal or lake. Seasonal feasts are, for our hard-working people, the only breaks in their daily toil!'

'The local people,' Dr Pien observed, 'believe that the boat races please the River Goddess, and ensure sufficient rain for the farmers and plenty of fish for the fishermen.' He fingered the black moustache that set off the pallor of his long, impassive face.

'In the olden days,' Mr Kou said, 'this feast was not so innocent, of course. The people used to make a human sacrifice after the races, killing a young man in the temple of the goddess. The "Groom of the Goddess" he was called, and the family of the victim considered that a signal honour.'

'Fortunately our enlightened government has abolished all those cruel customs centuries ago,' Judge Dee remarked.

'Old beliefs don't die easily,' Dr Pien said slowly. 'The people here still venerate the River Goddess, even though the Canal has now become much more important for fishing and shipping than the river. I remember that when, four years ago, a boat overturned during the races, and a man drowned, the local people took it as a good omen, promising a plentiful harvest in autumn.'

Kou gave the doctor an uneasy look. He put down his cup, rose and said:

'By Your Honour's leave, we'll now proceed to the grand-stand and see that everything is ready for the distribution of the prizes.'

Dr Pien got up also. They took their leave with low bows.

15

Judge Dee's three wives quickly came out from behind the screen and resumed their seats. The Third Lady glanced at the pieces in the pool, and said eagerly:

'There aren't many left. Now for the last struggle!'

The maids brought fresh tea. Soon the four were immersed in the game. Slowly stroking his long black beard, Judge Dee calculated his chances. His last domino was a three and a blank. All the threes had come out already, but there must be one double-blank left. If that came out, he had won. Watching the flushed faces of his wives, he was wondering idly who had that particular domino.

Suddenly there was a loud explosion near by, followed by a rattle of sharp cracks.

'Make your move!' the judge said impatiently to his Second Lady, who was sitting on his right. 'They are starting with the fireworks!'

She hesitated, patting her glossy black coiffure. Then she put a double four on the table.

'Pass!' Judge Dee said, disappointed.

'I win!' the Third Lady called out excitedly. She showed her last domino, a four and a five.

'Congratulations!' the judge exclaimed. Then he asked: 'Which of you had been saving up double-blank? I had been waiting for that confounded domino!'

'Not me!' his First and Second Lady announced as they uncovered their dominoes.

'That's strange!' Judge Dee said with a frown. 'There's only one double-blank on the table, and there's nothing left in the pool. Where can that domino have gone to?'

'It'll have dropped on the floor,' the First Lady said.

They looked under the table, then shook out their robes. But the domino did not appear.

'Perhaps the maids forgot to put it in the box,' the Second Lady said.

'Impossible!' the judge muttered crossly. 'When I took the pieces from the box before we started our game, I counted them. I always do.'

There was a hiss, followed by a sharp crack. The Canal was lit up by the shower of coloured lights that descended from the rocket.

'Look!' the First Lady exclaimed. 'What a beautiful sight!'

They quickly got up and went to stand at the railing. Rockets were being sent up now on all sides, and there was a constant rattle of fire-crackers. Then there rose a mighty roar from the crowd of spectators. The bleak, silvery light of the moon sickle had appeared in the sky. Now the race boats would leave Marble Bridge Village, a few miles down the Canal. There were some isolated cracks, then there was only a confused murmur of voices. People were eagerly discussing their bets.

'Let's make our bets too!' Judge Dee said good-humouredly. 'Every citizen, even the poorest, bets a few coppers.'

The Third Lady clapped her hands.

'I'll put fifty coppers on Number Three!' she called out. Just to show the God of Chance that I haven't forgotten him!'

'I'll put fifty on Dr Pien's boat, the favourite!' the First Lady said.

'And I'll put fifty on Kou's,' Judge Dee added. 'I believe in supporting tradition!'

They laughed and joked for some time, and thereafter had several leisurely cups of tea.

Suddenly they noticed that people were standing up in the boats, craning their heads to the bend in the Canal where, presently, the dragonboats would appear on their final lap to the finish. Judge Dee and his wives went up to

17

the railing again. The tense atmosphere of eager expectation was beginning to get hold of them too.

Two sampans detached themselves from the mass of moored craft. They were rowed to the centre of the Canal, opposite the grandstand. The occupants anchored them there and unfurled large red flags. They were the referees.

Suddenly the sound of drums was heard far off. The still-invisible boats were now approaching the bend.

The crowd broke out in a roar of confused shouts. Boat Number Nine was rounding the bend. The long, slender craft was propelled by twelve rowers, seated two abreast. They were moving their paddles vigorously to the beats of the large kettledrum in the middle of the boat. A tall, broad-shouldered man, stripped to the waist, was beating the drum frantically with a pair of wooden clubs. The helmsman, crouching over the long rudder-oar, shouted at the rowers at the top of his voice. White foam spurted up against the raised bow, carved to resemble a dragon's head with long horns and rolling eyes.

'That's Pien's boat! I win!' the First Lady shouted.

But when the stern, shaped like a curved dragon's tail, came in sight the bow of a second boat appeared close behind it; the raised dragon's head with its distended jaws seemed intent on putting its teeth into the tail of Number Nine.

'That's Number Two, manned by the boatmen of the Canal,' Judge Dee remarked. 'They are doing their best!'

The drummer of Number Two, a small, wiry man, was beating his drum in a frenzy, shouting encouragement at the crew all the time. As the boats came closer, Number Two gained on Nine, its dragon-head now by the side of the other's tail. The sound of the drums was nearly drowned in the deafening shouts of the spectators.

Four more boats had appeared round the bend, but no one paid any attention to them, all eyes were glued to

18

Nine and Two. The muscular arms of the rowers of Number Two moved with incredible speed, but they gained no more on Number Nine. The two boats were quite near now, Judge Dee could see the broad grin on the face of the big drummer of Number Nine. Now they were only a hundred yards from the finish. The referees lowered the red flags to mark the finishing-line.

Suddenly the big drummer of Nine checked his movement. The right club remained raised in the air. He seemed to look at it, astonished, for a moment, then he pitched forward over the drum. The rowers behind him looked up; two paddles clashed. The boat listed and slowed down. Number Nine and Two passed underneath the red flags together, but Number Two was half a boat-length ahead.

'Poor fellow collapsed.' Judge Dee began. 'They shouldn't drink so much before . . .' His voice was drowned in the deafening applause of the crowd. While Nine and Two were pulling up alongside the quay in front of the grandstand, the other seven dragonboats passed the finish, each greeted by the tremendous applause of the excited spectators. Fireworks started again on all sides.

The judge saw a large, official barge being rowed across towards their boat. Turning to his ladies he said:

'They are coming to fetch me for the distribution of the prizes. The steward will see you home in our palankeen. I'll follow as soon as the ceremony is over!'

His three ladies bowed, and he descended on the lower deck. Pien and Kou were waiting for him at the gangway. As he stepped on board the barge the judge said to the former:

'I am sorry that your boat lost, Dr Pien. I hope that the drummer is not seriously ill.'

'I'll go and have a look presently, sir. He's a strong fellow, we'll revive him all right. It was a fine race!'

Kou Yuan-liang said nothing, he nervously pulled at his

thin moustache. He started to say something, but changed his mind.

When they had arrived on the quay the headman of the constables, with six of his men, saluted the judge. Pien and Kou led him up the stairs of the grandstand. He was received on the platform by Sergeant Hoong, his faithful old assistant, who conducted him to a small dressing-room made of bamboo screens. As Hoong helped the judge to don his official robe of green brocade, Judge Dee said contentedly:

'It was a most enjoyable outing, Hoong!' Putting the winged judge's cap of black velvet on his head, he asked: 'Nothing happened in the tribunal, I suppose?'

'Only a few routine affairs, Your Honour,' the greybeard replied. 'I could let the clerks go home before six. They were very happy, for they could be here just in time to watch the races.'

'Good! While I am addressing the crowd, you had better go down to the quay and find out how that drummer of Boat Nine is doing. The poor wretch collapsed just before his boat reached the finish.'

Judge Dee stepped out on to the platform.

A large crowd had assembled down below. The constables had lined up the crews of the dragonboats at the bottom of the stairs. The headman took the leader of each boat up to the platform, where Judge Dee said a few kind words and handed out packages wrapped up in red paper. Each contained a small rice cake and a trifling sum of money.

Thereafter the judge made a brief speech, wishing all citizens good luck and prosperity during the rest of the year. He re-entered the dressing-room, loudly applauded by the crowd.

Sergeant Hoong was waiting for him. He said worriedly:

'The drummer is dead, sir. Our coroner says that he has been poisoned.'

III

Judge Dee looked down silently at the still figure of the dead drummer. The corpse had been brought up to the dressing-room and laid out on a reed mat on the floor. The coroner of the tribunal was squatting beside it. He had been standing among the spectators on the quay watching the finish, and had cursorily examined the body directly after it was brought on land. Now he was conducting a closer examination. He had inserted a silver stave into the mouth.

Dr Pien, who had been standing in a corner with Kou Yuan-liang, came forward and said in an irritated voice:

'This is a waste of time, Your Honour! I am certain he had a heart attack. All the symptoms point that way.'

'Let my coroner finish!' Judge Dee spoke curtly. He studied the dead man's muscular body, stripped to a loin cloth. The face was distorted by the death grimace, but the regular features and the smooth, broad forehead seemed to point to an educated man rather than to a shop assistant or a coolie—the class of people the crews were usually recruited from. As the coroner righted himself, the judge asked him:

'What made you think the man was poisoned? You have heard that Dr Pien believes that he died from a heart-attack.'

'In addition to the symptoms of heart failure, Your Honour, there are small purplish spots on the tips of the fingers and toes, and I verified just now that the tongue is swollen and covered by dark stains. I happen to be from the south, and I know that the mountain people there concoct a slow-working poison that produces exactly those symptoms. As soon as I had seen the spots on his finger-tips, I knew that he must have been killed by that particular poison.'

Dr Pien bent over the corpse. The coroner opened the mouth wide with the silver stave and let the doctor look inside. Pien nodded. He said contritely to the judge:

'Your coroner is quite right, sir. I was wrong. I now remember having read about that poison. If taken on an empty stomach, it will become effective after a quarter of an hour or so. But if taken after a heavy meal, it may take an hour or more.'

'Since he was the drummer of your boat, I take it that he was an employee of yours?'

'No, sir, he was a vagrant student; Tong Mai his name was. Occasionally he helped out as a clerk in my pharmacy, in the busy season.'

'Did he have no family here?'

'He did, sir, until a few years ago. He lived with his parents in a rather nice villa, in the countryside. Then his father had bad luck in business and lost all his money. He sold the house and moved back to their native place, up north. Tong Mai stayed behind in Poo-yang, hoping to scrape up enough to keep him going till he had completed his course in Classical Literature in the Temple of Confucius here, then join his parents up north. He was a cheerful, easy-going fellow, and also an excellent sportsman. Good amateur boxer, as a matter of fact. All my employees liked him, that is why they asked him to act as drummer of our boat.'

He cast a regretful look at the prone figure.

'Tong was quite a useful young man,' Mr Kou spoke up. 'His father knew a great deal about antiques, and Tong too had quite an eye for spotting a good thing.'

'How did you come to know him, Mr Kou?' Judge Dee asked.

'He often came to see me, sir, bringing a piece of porcelain or an old bronze that he had picked up cheaply. I agree with Dr Pien that he was a nice young fellow.'

'That did not prevent somebody from murdering him,' the judge remarked dryly. 'Was there anyone who could have harboured a grudge against him?'

Dr Pien gave Mr Kou a questioning look. When the latter shrugged his shoulders the doctor replied: 'Not that we know of, Your Honour. I must add, however, that Tong used to associate with queer people, vagabonds and hangers-on who frequent cheap boxing clubs. Perhaps a quarrel with one of those rascals . . .' He did not complete his sentence.

Pien was looking pale and nervous. Judge Dee reflected that the sudden death of his part-time employee seemed to have shocked him greatly. Or it might have been his wrong diagnosis that had upset the doctor. He asked Mr Kou: 'Where did Tong live?'

'Somewhere near Halfmoon Street, sir, in the south-west corner of the city. I don't know the exact address, but I can ask his friend Sia Kwang. Sia is also a vagrant student, and also an amateur boxer, and he too dabbled in the curio trade as a side line. Sia once told me that he and Tong shared an attic over the shop of an old-clothes merchant. Sia promised to help put away my boat, he must be around somewhere.'

'Have that youngster brought up here!' Judge Dee told the coroner.

'He has gone back to the city already, sir,' Dr Pien said quickly. 'I happened to see him just before I came up here, making for the south gate. Couldn't miss him, with that ugly scar across his left cheek.'

'That's a pity,' Judge Dee remarked. He saw that Kou Yuan-liang seemed eager to go, he was shifting impatiently from one foot to the other. 'Well, gentlemen,' he resumed, 'I shall make careful inquiries into this matter. Do not let it become known that Tong was murdered, for the time being. Call it heart failure. I shall expect both of you at the session of the tribunal tomorrow morning. While you are seeing these two gentlemen down, Hoong, tell our headman to come up here, will you.'

After Pien and Kou had taken their leave, the judge said to the coroner:

'I am glad to see that you know your job. If you hadn't happened to be there, I should have dismissed this murder as an accident, on Dr Pien's authority. You may go back to the tribunal now and draw up your report on the autopsy.'

The coroner left, smiling contentedly. Judge Dee started to pace the floor, his hands clasped behind his back. When Sergeant Hoong came back with the headman, he ordered the latter: 'Fetch me the dead man's clothes!'

'They are right here, sir.' The headman took a bundle from under the table and opened it. 'These are the trousers and belt he was wearing, Your Honour, and the pair of felt shoes he had on. And this, here, is his jacket, found folded up under the drum on his boat.'

Judge Dee put his hand in the capacious sleeve of the jacket and brought out an identity card made out to Tong Mai, a certificate stating that Tong Mai had passed his first literary examination, and two silver pieces wrapped up in tissue-paper. Replacing everything he told Hoong: 'Take these clothes to the tribunal.' And, to the headman: 'Have the body wrapped up in that mat, and let your men bring it to an empty cell in our jail. You yourself go to Tong Mai's lodging and take Sia Kwang to the tribunal. I'll question him later tonight.'

The headman left to call the constables. While Sergeant Hoong was helping the judge to take off his ceremonial robe, he asked:

'Who could have murdered that student? One would think that . . .'

24

'Murder?' a deep voice spoke up behind them. 'I was told it was an accident!'

The judge turned round with an angry remark on his lips. But he checked himself as he saw the huge man who was standing in the door opening. It was Yang, the curio-dealer who owned a large shop opposite the Temple of Confucius. The judge often went there to look over his antiques. He said, not unkindly:

'It was indeed murder, Mr Yang. But I must request you to keep this to yourself.'

The giant raised his bushy eyebrows. He had a strongly-featured, sun-tanned face, with a bristling moustache and a short beard. He said, with a slow smile that bared his white, even teeth:

'As you say, sir! I came to have a look because the fisher-men down at the quay are saying that the White Woman took him.'

'What do they mean by that?' Judge Dee asked testily.

'That's what the countryfolk call the River Goddess, sir. The fishermen are glad that a man died during the races, they say that, now that the goddess has got her due, there'll be plenty of fish this year.'

Judge Dee shrugged his shoulders.

'For the time being we'll let the murderer think that the authorities share the popular belief,' he said.

'How was he murdered, Your Honour?' Yang cast a quick glance at the prone figure, then added: 'I don't see any blood.'

'If you want the details, you'll have to attend the session of the tribunal tomorrow morning,' Judge Dee said curtly. 'By the way, since Tong Mai dabbled in the antique trade, I suppose you knew him well?'

Yang shook his large head.

'Knew of him sir. I never met him. I have my own

channels of supply! Got those by hard work, too! Riding up and down the countryside, rain or shine, always after farmers who dig up old stuff in their fields. Keeps me healthy, and well supplied with good, genuine articles. The other day——'

'Ever meet Tong's friend, fellow called Sia Kwang?'

'No sir. Sorry I can't oblige.' Yang wrinkled his corrugated brow. 'The name sounds familiar, somehow, but that's all. Well, as I was saying, the other day I got in a temple east of the city an old painting that Your Honour would be interested in, I dare say. It's in good condition, I——'

'One of these days I'll pass by your shop, Mr Yang. I am in rather a hurry now, I must go back to the tribunal.'

The curio-dealer bowed and took his leave.

'I like to chat with Yang,' the Judge remarked to Sergeant Hoong. 'The man has an uncanny knowledge of antiques. Has a genuine love for them, too. But he came at a most inopportune moment.' He put a small black skull-cap on his head and resumed, with a wan smile: 'Since my three lieutenants won't be back in Poo-yang until the day after tomorrow, we'll have to solve this murder the two of us, Hoong!'

'It's a pity that Ma Joong and Chiao Tai took Tao Gan along on their holiday, sir!' the sergeant said wistfully. 'That sly fellow is just the man for solving a case of poisoning!'

'Don't worry, we'll manage, Hoong! I'll now take a horse and ride to Marble Bridge Village. Evidently the poison was put into Tong Mai's food or drink while the crews were being entertained there before the races. I shall have a look at things out there. I want you to go to the Temple of Confucius and see the Director of Studies, old Professor Ou-yang. Ask him about Tong Mai, and also about his friend Sia Kwang. The professor is a shrewd old fellow, I'd like to have his opinion on the character of those two young men. You needn't wait up for me, I'll see you tomorrow morning after breakfast, in my private office.

While they were going down the stairs together, the judge added:

'Oh yes, pass by my residence, will you, and let the steward inform my ladies that I shall be in later tonight.'

IV

Judge Dee took the horse of one of the constables, swung himself into the saddle and rode off, heading south. The highway was crowded with people from up-country going home, they paid no attention to the solitary horseman galloping by.

The highway followed the Canal for about one mile. Small groups of men and women were still sitting on the bank, from which they had been watching the races. Then he entered the hills. There dark woods rose on either side of the road. When he had descended into the plain again he saw the coloured lights of the street-stalls that marked the entrance of Marble Bridge Village. Crossing the high curved bridge that had given the village its name, he saw the masts of the large river junks moored at the quay farther along, at the confluence of the river and the Grand Canal.

The market-place on the other side of the bridge was glittering with hundreds of oil-lamps and lampions. A dense crowd was milling around the stalls. Judge Dee dismounted and led his horse by the bridle to the shop of a blacksmith. The man had little to do, he agreed to look after the horse for a few coppers. The judge noticed with satisfaction that the blacksmith did not recognize him as the magistrate.

He strolled along, looking for a likely place to gather information. Under the high trees on the river-bank he saw the red-lacquered pillars of a small shrine. He joined the stream of people that filed past it. Each dropped a few coppers in the offering-box that stood at the head of the stone steps leading up to the sanctuary. While contributing his coppers Judge Dee looked curiously inside. An aged

Taoist priest, clad in a tattered brown cowl, was adding new oil to the single lamp that hung over the altar. On it he saw a life-size statue of the River Goddess, sitting cross-legged on her lotus-throne. The half-closed eyes seemed to be looking down on him, her lips were curved in a faint smile.

As a staunch Confucianist Judge Dee had little patience with the idolatrous popular cults. Yet the beautiful smiling face gave him a strange feeling of disquiet. With an angry shrug he went down the stairs and walked on. A little farther along he saw a barber's stall. Its open front faced the waterfront. As he entered and sat down on the low tabouret, his eye fell on a slender woman who had detached herself from the crowd and now came walking towards the stall. She wore an outer robe of black damask, and the lower half of her face was covered by a black scarf wound round her head. She could hardly be a prostitute, her quiet attire and her proud bearing clearly indicated a person of standing. While taking off his skull-cap, he vaguely wondered what could have brought an unattended lady to this noisy market at such a late hour. Then he concentrated on detailed instructions to the barber as to how he wanted his beard and whiskers trimmed.

'Where might you be hailing from, sir?' the barber asked as he began to comb out Judge Dee's beard.

'I am a boxing-master from the neighbouring district,' the judge replied. He knew that boxing-masters, their profession compelling them to live in an austere manner, were highly regarded by the people—the kind of persons that invite confidences. He added: 'I am on my way to the capital to visit my relatives. You must have been doing good business tonight, with all those people about here for the races.'

'Not too good, to tell you the truth! People had better

things to think of than having their hair cut, you know. See that large wine-house over on the opposite bank there? Before the boats took off, the Hon'ble Pien and Kou entertained the rowers there, and all their friends and relatives too. Now, I ask you, who is going to spend good coppers on his hair when he can eat a snack and drink his fill, all free for nothing?'

Judge Dee agreed that that was true. Out of the corner of his eye he saw the woman in black standing close by the balustrade that separated the barber's shop from the street. Perhaps she was a prostitute after all, waiting there to accost him when he left. He said to the barber:

'I see only four waiters in the wine-house over there. They must have had a busy time serving all those rowers! I heard that there were nine dragonboats this time.'

'No, they didn't! Do you see that table in the back? Well, they had put six large wine-jars there. Each and everyone could dip in his bowl as often as he liked! And those two side-tables were heaped with cold snacks. Help yourself! Seeing that I have a couple of clients among the rowers, I thought I was more or less entitled to join the guests, and I hopped over myself. I can tell you that they served nothing but the best, sir! The Hon'ble Pien and Kou don't grudge expense when they entertain, no sir they don't! Not a bit stuck up either, they were up and about all the time, had a kind word for everyone. Do you want to have your hair washed?' As the judge shook his head the barber went on: 'Our villagers will go on drinking till midnight, I wager, even though they'll have to pay for it now! There was an accident during the races, you know, a fellow died. That's why everybody here is glad. For now that the White One has got her due, there'll be good crops this autumn!'

'Do you believe in the White Woman?'

'Well, sir, I do and I don't, so to speak. My trade not

depending on the water or the field, I can afford to keep an open mind in the matter, more or less, you see. But I wouldn't willingly go near that Mandrake Grove up there, sir!' He pointed with his scissors and added: 'For that belongs to her, and I believe in keeping on the safe side!'

'I too, so stop waving those scissors around my head, man! That'll do fine, thank you. How much do I owe you?'

He paid his coppers, put on his skull-cap, and went out.

The woman in black stepped up to him and said curtly:

'I would like to have a word with you.'

Judge Dee halted and gave her a sharp look. Her cultured voice and air of assurance confirmed his first impression that she was indeed a lady. She went on quickly:

'I heard you say just now that you are a boxing-master. I might have work for you tonight.'

The judge was curious to know what this strange woman wanted. He said:

'I am travelling, and travelling costs money. I could do with something extra.'

'Follow me!'

She walked over to the rustic stone seats under the willows along the waterside and sat down. Judge Dee took the seat opposite. She let down her veil and looked steadily at him for a while with her large, gleaming eyes. She was a remarkably beautiful woman. Her almond-shaped face was not made up, but her delicate small mouth had a natural, bright-red colour, and a slight blush enlivened her smooth cheeks. He put her age at about twenty-five. Her scrutiny completed, she resumed:

'You seem to be a decent fellow, I don't think you'll take undue advantage of the situation. Well, it's quite simple, really. I agreed to meet someone, for an important trans-action, in a deserted house near the Mandrake Grove, about half an hour's walk from here. But, when I made the appoint-

31

AN ENCOUNTER BY THE WATERSIDE

ment, I stupidly overlooked the fact that on the night of the dragonboat races all kinds of riff-raff are about here. I want you to accompany me to the house, to protect me against footpads and so on. You only need to bring me up to the gate.' She felt in her sleeve, brought out a shining silver piece, and added: 'I am prepared to pay you well for this slight service.'

The judge thought he must certainly know more about this. So he rose abruptly and said coldly:

'I am not more averse to easy money than the next. But I am a boxing-master with an established reputation, and I refuse to connive at clandestine meetings.'

'How dare you!' she exclaimed angrily. 'All this is quite above board, I tell you!'

'You'll have to prove that first, if you want my help.'

'Sit down! Time is pressing, I'll have to humour you. And your reluctance confirms my favourable impression of you. Now then, I am commissioned to buy tonight an object of great value. The price has been agreed upon, but special circumstances make it necessary that the transaction be kept secret. There are others who want the same thing, and the owner can't afford for them to know that he is selling to me. He is waiting for me now in that house. It has been deserted for years, one couldn't imagine a safer place for a confidential transaction involving a considerable amount of money.'

Judge Dee looked at her sagging left sleeve.

'Do you mean to say,' he asked, 'that you, a woman and all alone, are carrying the purchasing price on you in cash?'

She took a square package from her left sleeve and silently handed it to him. After having made sure that no one was looking at them, he pried a corner of the thick paper loose. Involuntarily he gasped. It contained ten shining gold bars, packed close together. Returning it to her, he asked:

33

'Who are you?'

'You see that I trust you completely,' she replied calmly as she put the package back into her sleeve. 'I expect the same from you.' Taking out the silver piece again she asked: 'Is it a deal?'

The judge nodded and accepted the silver piece. His conversation with the barber had made it clear that searching here for a clue to Tong Mai's poisoning was a hopeless task. The next day he would have to make a thorough inquiry into the background and relations of the murdered man, in order to discover a clue to the motive of the crime. There was no sense in going farther into the question of opportunity, for anybody could have put the poison in his wine or food during the entertainment in the wine-house. He might as well see now what this strange woman was up to. As they were crossing the market together he said:

'I'd better buy a storm-lantern here.'

'I know that property like the palm of my hand!' she said impatiently.

'But I don't, and I'll have to find my way back alone,' the judge remarked dryly. He halted at a stall where household goods were sold and bought a small lantern made of oil-paper stretched over a bamboo frame. When they were walking on, he asked, curiously: 'How did the fellow you are going to meet find his way out there?'

'He used to live in that house. And he'll see me back to the village—in case you are worrying about that!'

They went on in silence. After they had entered the dark road leading up to the forest, they passed a group of young hooligans who were romping there with three streetwalkers. They began to make ribald remarks about the passing pair. But, after a second look at Judge Dee's tall frame, they stopped abruptly.

A little farther on the woman left the road and entered a

34

pathway leading into the wood. They met two vagabonds who were hovering about under the trees. They came for them, but, when they saw the judge folding back his sleeves with the self-assured gesture of the experienced boxer, they quickly walked on. Judge Dee reflected that at least he was earning his pay. All alone the woman would never have reached her destination unmolested.

Soon he could not hear the noise of the market any more, the stillness was broken only by the eerie cries of the night-jar. The winding path led through a dense forest of high trees, whose branches met overhead so that only small patches of moonlight filtered through to the ground, covered by a thick layer of dry leaves.

The woman turned round and pointed to a tall, gnarled pine tree.

'Remember this tree,' she said. 'On your way back you turn to the left here, and keep to the left.'

She took a footpath, overgrown with weeds. She seemed to be completely familiar with it, but the judge had difficulty in keeping up with her without stumbling on the uneven ground. To gain time for a brief rest he asked:

'Why was this property deserted?'

'Because they thought it was haunted. It borders on the Mandrake Grove, and you heard what that fool of a barber said. Are you a coward?'

'Not more than most.'

'Good. Keep quiet then, we are nearly there.'

After what seemed to him an interminable walk she stood still. She laid her hand on his arm and pointed ahead. The treetops were farther apart there; he saw in the bleak moonlight a gatehouse of weatherbeaten bricks. On either side was a high wall. She went up the three steps that led to a heavy double door of mouldering wood, pushed it open and whispered:

'Many thanks and goodbye!'

She slipped inside.

Judge Dee turned round and walked away. But as soon as he was behind the trees again he halted. He put the lantern on the ground, tucked the slips of his long robe under his belt and rolled up his sleeves. Then he took up the lantern again and made for the gatehouse. He would locate the meeting-place of the mysterious pair, and find a corner of vantage from where he could watch them. If it were indeed a straightforward business deal he would leave at once. But, should there be any cause for suspicion, he would make his presence known, reveal his identity, and demand a full explanation.

As soon as he had gone inside, however, he realized that his task would not be as easy as he had imagined, for the country house was not built according to the usual plan. Instead of coming out on an open front courtyard, he found himself in a kind of dark tunnel. Not wanting to light the lantern, he felt his way along the moss-covered stone wall, making for the faint light that shimmered ahead.

Having passed through the tunnel, he came out on a large, neglected yard. Weeds grew among the broken stone paving. On the other side loomed the dark mass of the main building, its partly caved in rooftops outlined against the moonlit sky. He crossed the yard, then stopped. He thought he had heard a vague noise on his right, where a narrow door opening seemed to lead to the east wing. He quickly passed through it and listened. Voices were coming from a square pavilion raised on a base about four feet high, on the other side of a small, walled-in garden, overgrown with weeds. The walls and roof of the pavilion were in a better state of repair than the rest of the compound. The door was tightly closed, and the single window shuttered. The voices came through the open transom over the entrance. Judge

Dee quickly studied the situation. The outer wall on his left was only four feet high, beyond it rose the tall trees of the dark forest. The wall on his right was higher. He thought that if he climbed on top he would be able to hear and see what was going on inside through the open transom.

He selected a spot where the crumbling bricks offered a fairly easy ascent. But, when he was crouching on top of the wall, the moon was clouded over and everything became pitch dark. He crept towards the pavilion as quickly as he dared. He heard the woman say:

'I won't tell you anything until I know why you are here.'

There was an oath, then the sounds of a scuffle. The woman cried:

'Keep your hands off, I tell you!'

At that moment part of the wall gave way under Judge Dee's weight. While he steadied himself with difficulty, a mass of bricks crashed down into the rubble below. As he was groping among the broken bricks for a hold to let himself down, he suddenly heard the woman scream. Then there was the sound of a door being opened, and of hurried footsteps. He let himself drop among the shrubs at the foot of the wall and shouted:

'Stay where you are, my men have surrounded the house!'

It was the best he could think of, but it was evidently not good enough. As he scrambled up he heard the sound of breaking branches far ahead, near the gatehouse. The fugitive was escaping into the wood.

The judge looked at the pavilion. Through the half-open door he could see part of the interior, lit by a single candle. The woman in black was lying on the floor.

He stumbled through the weeds and rushed up the stone steps. He halted in the door opening. She was lying on her

B*

back, the hilt of a dagger sticking up from her breast. He quickly squatted down by her side and intently studied the still face. She was dead.

'She paid me to protect her, and I let her be murdered!' he muttered angrily.

Apparently she had tried to defend herself, for a long thin knife was clasped in her right hand. The blade was stained with blood, and a trail of red drops led across the floor to the door.

He put his hand into her sleeve. The package with the gold bars was gone. There were only two handkerchiefs, and a receipted bill made out to 'The Amber Lady, the Hon'ble Kou Yuan-liang's mansion'. Judge Dee looked again at the still, pale face. He remembered having heard people say that Kou's First Lady had been suffering for years from an incurable disease and that Kou had taken unto him a beautiful young woman and installed her as his Second Lady. This must be she. That fool of a Kou had sent her here all alone to purchase some valuable antique for his collection! But it had been a trap, to steal the gold.

With a sigh he rose and inspected the bare room. He knitted his eyebrows in a puzzled frown. Next to the chair, the only piece of furniture was a bamboo couch. There were no cupboards or wall niches, no place to store away anything. The walls and ceiling had been recently repaired, and the window provided with solid iron bars. The door consisted of thick new boards and had a large iron lock. Perplexedly shaking his head, he took the candle up and lighted his lantern with it. Then he descended into the walled-in garden again and walked over to the main building.

Not a stick of furniture was left in the dark, damp rooms. In the half-ruined main hall his eye fell on an inscription engraved in the plaster of the back wall. The two large

38

letters read 'River Villa'. They were signed by the name Tong I-kwan.

'Good calligraphy!' he muttered as he continued his tour of the house. In the empty corridors a few bats came fluttering round his head, attracted by the light of his lantern. But apart from those and a few large rats that scurried away on his approach all was silent as the grave.

He walked back to the pavilion to collect the two knives. Then he would return to Marble Bridge and order the village headman to come with his men and bring the dead woman to the city. There was nothing he could do here in this dismal place. When he entered the walled-in garden he saw that the moon had come out again.

Suddenly he stood stock-still. Somebody was walking stealthily along the other side of the low wall that separated the garden from the forest. He saw only the intruder's tousled head, moving away from the pavilion. Evidently he had not heard the judge, for he unhurriedly continued his progress.

Judge Dee crouched and stepped noiselessly up to the low wall. Grabbing its top he vaulted over and landed in a kind of ditch, overgrown with wild plants. Scrambling up he saw that on this side the wall rose more than six feet above the narrow bank of the ditch. No one was there.

He looked up at the wall and froze in nameless terror. The tousled head was creeping along the top of the wall all by itself, with strange, jerky moves.

He stood breathless for a moment, his eyes fixed on that horrible thing. Then he smiled suddenly, and heaved a deep sigh of relief. The moonlight had played him a trick. It was just a bunch of tangled weeds, being dragged along by some small animal or other.

He reached up and pulled the weeds apart. The small land tortoise underneath gave the judge a reproachful look from its opaque eyes, then quickly drew its head and legs inside its shell.

'A wise policy, my little friend!' Judge Dee muttered. 'Wish I could do the same!'

It was a comfort to talk. The forbidding atmosphere of this strange place was beginning to oppress him. He cast an uneasy glance at the black mass of the wood, rising on the other side of the ditch from a solid wall of thick undergrowth. This evidently was the Mandrake Grove, sacred to the River Goddess. Not a leaf was stirring in the silvery moonlight.

'This is no place for us,' the judge addressed the tortoise. 'You'd better come with me. You are just what I needed for enlivening my small rock-garden. The White One won't miss you, I trust!'

He took out his handkerchief and laid the tortoise on it. Having knotted the ends together, he put it in his sleeve. Then he climbed over the wall again, and back into the garden.

He went once more inside the pavilion and carefully pulled the dagger from the woman's breast. It had penetrated straight into her heart, and the front of the black dress was soaked with blood. Then he took the other knife from her lifeless hand and wrapped both weapons in one of her handkerchiefs. He gave the room a last look, and left.

Arrived at the gatehouse, he studied the tunnel. He now saw also that a parapet ran all along the top of the outer wall. Evidently the owner of this lonely villa had fortified the approaches, fearing attacks by bandit bands. He shrugged his shoulders and left the villa. Aided by his lantern, he found the way back to Marble Bridge without difficulty.

The market still presented a gay scene. The villagers were not thinking yet of turning in. He ordered a loafer to take him to the village headman. He told the headman who he was, and gave the frightened man instructions about the corpse. He also ordered him to post a dozen or so militia in the villa, to stand guard till daybreak. Then he fetched his horse from the blacksmith, put the two daggers and the tortoise in his saddle-bag and rode back to the city.

V

The soldiers on guard at the south gate were keeping the huge, iron-bound door ajar. Small groups of citizens were still coming in, despite the advanced hour. Each handed the corporal a marker, a small oblong piece of bamboo with a number scrawled on it. Every citizen wishing to re-enter the city after closing time had to ask for such a marker on leaving. People without a marker were admitted only after having paid a fine of five coppers, and after having given their name, profession and address.

When the corporal recognized the judge, he barked at the soldiers to open the gate wide at once. Judge Dee halted his horse. He asked:

'Did a wounded man enter the gate a while ago?'

The corporal pushed his helmet back from his moist brow and replied unhappily:

'I really couldn't say, Excellency! We had no time to look every man up and down, the crowd . . .'

'All right. From now on you'll examine every man carefully for a recent knife wound. If you find him, arrest him, no matter who he is, and bring him to the tribunal at once. Send one of your soldiers on horseback to the three other city gates and transmit the same order to your colleagues on duty there!'

Then he rode on. The streets were still filled by a merry crowd, and the wine-houses and street-stalls were doing a brisk trade. The judge guided his horse to the east quarter. He remembered having heard that Kou Yuan-liang's house was located there. At the Garrison Headquarters he made inquiries with the captain of the guard, and an orderly conducted him to a large mansion in the quiet residential section not far from the east gate. While Judge Dee dismounted, the orderly knocked on the red-lacquered double front door.

As soon as the old gatekeeper had learned Judge Dee's identity, he hurried inside to apprise his master of the arrival of the distinguished guest. Mr Kou came rushing out into the front courtyard. He was in a state of great consternation. Forgetting the amenities, he asked excitedly:

'Was there an accident?'

'There was. Let's go inside, shall we?'

'Of course, sir! Please excuse me, sir, I am so . . .' Kou shook his head contritely, then led the judge through a winding corridor to a large library, sparsely furnished with a few solid antique pieces. When they were seated at the round tea-table in the corner Judge Dee asked:

'Is your Second Lady's personal name Amber?'

'Yes, Your Honour, indeed! What has happened to her? She left here on an errand directly after dinner, and she hasn't come back yet. What . . .'

He broke off as he saw the steward come in with the tea-tray. While Mr Kou poured out two cups, the judge studied his face, slowly caressing his side-whiskers. After Kou had sat down again he said gravely:

'I deeply regret to inform you, Mr Kou, that the Amber Lady was found murdered.'

Kou grew pale. He sat very still, fixing the judge with wide, frightened eyes. Suddenly he burst out:

'Murdered! How could that happen? Who did it? Where was she when . . .'

Judge Dee raised his hand.

'As to your last question, you know the answer to that, Mr Kou. For it was you who sent her to that lonely place.'

'Lonely place? What lonely place? Heavens, why didn't

43

she listen to me! I implored her to tell me at least where she was going, but she . . .'

'You had better begin at the beginning, Mr. Kou,' the judge interrupted him again. 'Here, drink a cup of tea first. This must be a terrible shock to you of course. But if I don't get all the details here and now, I'll never catch the villain who murdered her.'

Kou swallowed a few mouthfuls, then asked in a calmer voice:

'Who did it?'

'A man as yet unknown.'

'How was she killed?'

'By a dagger thrust into her heart. She didn't suffer, she died at once.'

Kou nodded slowly. He resumed in a soft voice:

'She was a remarkable woman, sir. She had an uncanny talent for judging antiques and, especially, precious stones. She always assisted me in my antiquarian studies, she was such a charming companion . . .' He looked forlornly at the shelves of carved blackwood that stood against the side wall to the right of the door and carried a tastefully arranged display of porcelain and jade pieces. 'All that was done by her,' he went on, 'and she also made the catalogue. When I bought her four years ago she was illiterate, but after I had taught her for a year or two she had learned to write a very good hand indeed . . .'

He broke off and buried his face in his hands.

'Where did you acquire her?' Judge Dee asked gently.

'She was a slave-maid in the house of old Mr Tong I-kwan. I——'

'Tong I-kwan?' Judge Dee exclaimed. That was the signature added to the inscription he had seen in the hall of the haunted house! And she had told him that she and the man she was going to meet there knew the property

44

thoroughly! He resumed: 'I take it that Tong I-kwan was the father of Tong Mai, the murdered student?'

'Indeed, sir. Amber was an orphan, and old Mrs Tong had grown quite fond of her. Four years ago, when Tong I-kwan was obliged to sell all his possessions, he wanted a good house for Amber, and offered her to me. Since I have no children, I bought her for four gold bars, intending to adopt her as my daughter. But she grew more beautiful every day; she had an exquisite grace, like that of a jade statue; she . . .' He rubbed his hand over his eyes. After a while he added: 'Since my First Lady is . . . has a chronic disease, two years ago I married Miss Amber, as my second wife. Of course I am somewhat older, but our common interests . . .'

'I quite understand. Now, what about that errand you sent her on?'

Kou slowly emptied his teacup before he replied:

'Well, it was like this, Your Honour. She had recommended Tong Mai to me as a useful person for hunting out antiques. She knew him well of course, because they had grown up together. Two days ago she told me that Tong Mai had come upon a very rare and extremely valuable antique, a . . . vase. That vase was one of the finest in existence, and the price was ten gold bars. She said it was really worth double that amount, or more. Since it was a famous piece, coveted by many other collectors, Tong didn't want it to become known that he was selling it to me. She said he had promised to hand it to her in a safe place, known to both of them. She would go there tonight, after the races. I tried to make her tell me where it was. A young woman all alone, carrying all that money. . . . But she insisted that it was absolutely safe. . . . Then, tonight, when I saw that Tong was dead, I knew that she would wait for him in vain. I had expected to find her back here already when I

45

came home. When she didn't come, I became worried. But I couldn't do anything, for I didn't even know where their meeting place was. . . .'

'I can tell you that,' Judge Dee said 'Their rendezvous was the deserted Tong mansion, in the forest near Marble Bridge Village. She did not know that Tong was dead. Another person who knew about the transaction went there in Tong's place. That person murdered her, and stole the money and the, ah . . . vase. It was a vase you said, wasn't it?'

'The deserted house! Almighty Heaven, why did she . . . Well, the place was familiar to her, of course, but . . .' He dropped his gaze.

Judge Dee gave his host a searching look. Then he asked:
'Why do people say that the house is haunted?'
Kou looked up, startled.
'Haunted? Oh, that is because of the Mandrake Grove, sir. Many centuries ago this area was a swampy, thickly-wooded region, you know, and the river was much broader than it is now. This district was the centre of the cult of the River Goddess. Fishermen and boatpeople used to come from far and near to worship her. The Mandrake Grove was a large forest at that time; in the middle stood a beautiful shrine with a colossal marble statue of the goddess. Every year a young man was sacrificed on the altar. Then, however, the Grand Canal was extended through this region, and the forest cleared. Only the grove surrounding the shrine was left untouched, in deference to the beliefs of the local people. But the government ordered the discontinuation of the human sacrifices. The next year there was a disastrous earthquake that destroyed part of the shrine, and during which the priest and his two acolytes were killed. The people said that the goddess was angry. Therefore they abandoned the shrine and built a new one, on the river-

bank in Marble Bridge Village. The pathways leading through the Mandrake Grove were soon overgrown, and no one has dared to enter that grove since. Not even the gatherers of herbs venture inside, although the roots of the mandrake that gave the grove its name are supposed to have powerful medicinal properties and fetch a high price on the drug market, as Your Honour knows.'

Kou frowned, he seemed to have lost the thread of his narrative. He cleared his throat a few times, refilled the teacups, and then went on:

'Well, ten years ago, when old Mr Tong began building his villa close by the Mandrake Grove, the local people warned him that it was sheer folly to disturb the neighbourhood of the sacred grove. They refused to work for him, saying that the White One would resent the intrusion, and that there would be droughts and other disasters if Tong did not desist. But old Tong was an obstinate fellow and, as a northerner, he did not believe in the goddess. He imported labour from another district and built his villa. He moved in with his entire family and stored there his collection of antique bronzes. I went to see him a few times and found his bronzes of exceptional quality. It's very hard to find good bronzes nowadays, you know, it's a great pity that . . .' His voice stopped mid-sentence. He sadly shook his head, then pulled himself together and resumed: 'One summer evening, four years ago, after a hot and sultry day, old Tong was enjoying with his family the cool evening air, sitting in the walled-in garden, in front of the East Pavilion. Then suddenly the White One appeared among the trees of the Mandrake Grove, right opposite them. Old Tong told me about it later; it was terrible. . . . She was naked under a white, blood-stained dress, and her long, wet hair was hanging over her face. Raising her claw-like hands covered with blood she came for them, uttering a piercing howl.

47

Tong and the others sprang up and ran away as fast as they could. The violent storm that had been threatening all that day suddenly broke loose, there were flashes of lightning and terrific thunderclaps, followed by torrential rain. When Tong and the members of his household came stumbling into the village, drenched to the skin and their clothes torn by the branches, they were more dead than alive.

'Old Tong decided of course to abandon the house at once. Moreover, the next day he heard that his firm in the capital had gone bankrupt. He sold the house and the land to a wealthy drug-dealer in the capital, and left.'

He broke off abruptly. Judge Dee had been listening intently, slowly stroking his long black beard. After a while he asked:

'Why did Miss Amber, who knew all this, still make bold to visit that haunted house at night?'

'She didn't believe that the house was really haunted, sir. She used to say that the ghostly apparition was nothing but a hoax, arranged by the local people to frighten Tong. Moreover, being a woman, she had no need to be afraid, really. The White Goddess stands for the mysterious, creative force of fertile nature, she is considered as the guardian of womanhood. Therefore only young men were sacrificed to her, never women or girls.'

The judge nodded. He took a few sips from his tea. As he set his cup down he suddenly addressed Kou sternly:

'You allowed the Amber Lady to go out on a dangerous errand on your behalf, and she was cruelly done to death. You bear the responsibility for this dastardly crime! Yet you dare to tell me a rigmarole about an antique vase! No, don't interrupt me. Do you really think I am so ignorant that I don't know there is no antique vase in the Empire that is worth a dozen gold bars? Speak up, and tell the truth! What was Miss Amber trying to buy for you?'

48

Kou jumped up. He paced the floor in great agitation. At last he seemed to have made up his mind. He halted in front of the judge. After having cast an anxious glance at the closed door, he bent over to him and whispered hoarsely:

'It was the Emperor's Pearl!'

VI

Judge Dee looked dumbfounded at his excited host. Then he hit his fist on the table and shouted:

'I ordered you, you fool, to tell the truth! And now you dare to foist on me that nonsense about the Emperor's Pearl! Holy Heaven, my nursemaid told me that as a bedtime story when I was still a small child! The Emperor's Pearl, forsooth!'

He tugged angrily at his beard.

Kou resumed his seat. He wiped his moist brow with the tip of his sleeve, then said earnestly:

'It's true, Your Honour, I swear it! Amber saw the pearl. It has the size of a dove's egg, is perfectly oval, and has that peerless white shine that was praised so much!'

'And what fancy tale did Tong Mai concoct about how he got the famous Imperial treasure into his hands?'

Leaning forward in his chair, Kou replied quickly:

'Tong got it from a destitute old crone who used to live near to his lodging, sir. He once did her a good turn, and on her deathbed she gave him the pearl, as a token of her gratitude. Since she had no relatives left she could at last disclose the terrible old secret her family had guarded all through two generations.'

'So now we have an old family secret too!' the judge said with a sigh. 'All right, let's hear it!'

'It's a curious story, sir, but it bears the hallmark of truth. The old crone's grandmother used to be a chambermaid in the Imperial seraglio. When her mother was only a child of three, the Persian Ambassador presented the famous pearl to the Illustrious Grandfather of our present Emperor, and

His Majesty gave it to the Empress, on her birthday. This truly imperial gift created a tremendous stir in the harem, all the court ladies were crowding round the Empress in her bedroom to congratulate her upon this new mark of the Emperor's love. The small girl who was playing on the terrace outside heard all the commotion. She slipped inside the room and saw the pearl, which was lying on a side-table, on a brocade cushion. She took it, put it into her mouth and went outside, planning to play with it in the garden. When the loss was discovered, the Empress summoned at once the eunuchs and the harem guards. All doors were locked, and everybody was searched. But nobody bothered about the small child that was running about in the park. Four court ladies whom the Empress suspected were tortured to death, scores of palace attendants severely flogged, but the pearl was not found, of course. The same night two Imperial Censors were ordered to institute a most thorough investigation.'

Kou's cheeks had reddened; in his excitement over this strange old tale he seemed to have momentarily forgotten his grief. He took a hasty sip from his tea, then resumed:

'The next morning the chambermaid noticed that her small daughter was sucking on something. When she scolded the child for having been at the jar of sweets again, she innocently showed her mother that it was the pearl. The woman was frantic. If she returned the pearl and told the truth, she and her entire family would be executed, being responsible for the death of four innocent people. So she held her peace, and hid the pearl.

'The investigation continued for days on end, the judges of the Metropolitan Court were ordered to assist the Censors. The Emperor promised large rewards for anyone who would be able to solve the riddle, and the incident became known all over the Empire. All kinds of theories were brought forward, but of course the pearl was never found.

'The maid kept the pearl till she felt her end approaching, then she gave it to the mother of the old crone, swearing her to silence. That woman married a carpenter who got into debt, and she lived in poverty till the end of her days. You can imagine the dire straits those people were in, sir! They held a fabulous treasure in their hands, but it was of no avail, for they could never turn it into cash. No dealer would dare to touch it, he would report to the authorities at once, with all the terrible consequences. As well as causing the death of four innocent women, the family was also guilty of robbing the Imperial House, and such a sacrilegious crime is brought home to those responsible till the third generation. On the other hand they could not bear to throw the pearl into a well or get rid of it in some other way. The pearl must have haunted the unfortunate owners! The old crone's husband died when she was still a young woman. Although she had to eke out a precarious existence as laundrywoman, she never dared to tell anybody about the treasure in her possession. It was only when all her relatives had died, and when she herself was mortally ill, that she took out the pearl and gave it to Tong Mai.'

Kou fell silent. He looked expectantly at the judge.

Judge Dee made no comment. He reflected that this could well be the perfectly simple solution of that century-old riddle over which the most ingenious brains had been puzzling for so long. The Empress surrounded by a bevy of excited court ladies, all dressed in their wide, trailing robes that billowed around them . . . one could well imagine that no one noticed the small child romping about on the floor. On the other hand it could also be just a cleverly made up fairy-tale. After a long silence he asked evenly:

'Why didn't Tong Mai take the pearl to the palace? The

court officials could easily check the lineage of the old woman, and if she was really descended from that chambermaid, they would give Tong a rich reward. Much more than your ten gold bars.'

'Tong was, after all, only a vagrant student, sir. He was afraid that the authorities would not believe his story, and put him to the torture. Thus it seemed a reasonable arrangement that he would get the ten gold bars, and I the credit of having restored this long-lost treasure to its rightful owner, our Imperial House.'

Judge Dee observed dubiously his host's virtuous expression. He felt inclined to doubt his last statement. Enthusiast collectors often had no morality at all. He thought it far more likely that Kou would have kept the pearl for himself, in order to gloat over it secretly for the rest of his life. He said coldly :

'You call it a reasonable arrangement. I call it criminal failure to report at once vital facts regarding a theft from the palace. You should have reported to me at once what the Amber Lady had told you. Now you have caused the loss of an Imperial treasure. I hope for you that it will prove to be only a temporary loss. I shall do what I can to trace the murderer and to recover the pearl. The pearl may then prove to be a fake, and the story a hoax—if you are lucky, that is! ' Cutting short Kou's stuttered questions by getting up abruptly, the judge resumed: 'One last question. Did Tong Mai tell you that he had repaired the pavilion of the old house, and used it for storing the curios he dealt in?'

'Never, sir ! Amber didn't know about that either, I am sure.'

'I see.' As Judge Dee was turning to the door he suddenly halted. A tall, stately woman was standing in the door opening.

53

Kou quickly went up to her. Laying his hand on her arm he spoke in a soft voice:

'You must go back to your room, Gold Lotus! You know you aren't well, dear!'

She did not seem to have heard him. As Judge Dee joined them he saw that she was about thirty, and of truly outstanding beauty. She had a thin, straight nose, a delicate small mouth and long, gracefully curved eyebrows. But the still face was curiously void of expression, the large lacklustre eyes were staring vacantly ahead. She wore a black silk robe with long, trailing sleeves, the broad sash set off to advantage her slender waist and her shapely bosom. Her glossy hair was combed back straight, and decorated only by a small lotus flower of gold-filigree.

'My First Lady's mind is deranged, Your Honour,' Kou whispered unhappily. 'She lost her reason after an attack of brain-fever, some years ago. She stays in her room most of the time, if she were to go out alone she might hurt herself. Her maids must have let her slip out, all the servants were so upset about Amber's disappearance, tonight . . .'

Bending over to his wife he murmured some endearing words. But she gave no sign that she was aware of his presence. Staring straight ahead she raised her slender white hand and slowly patted her hair.

Judge Dee gave the strange woman a pitying look. Then he said to Kou:

'Better look after her, I'll find my way out.'

VII

When Judge Dee halted his horse in front of the main gate of the tribunal, it was about one hour before midnight. He leaned forward in the saddle and knocked with the butt of his riding-whip on the iron-bound door. Two guards quickly pushed the heavy gate open, and the judge rode under the stone arch on to the central courtyard of the compound. While he was handing his horse to a sleepy-looking groom he saw a light burning behind the paper window of his private office, next to the court hall. He walked over there, carrying his saddle-bag with him.

Sergeant Hoong was sitting on a tabouret in front of Judge Dee's large writing-desk, reading a document by the light of the single candle. He quickly rose as he saw the judge coming in and asked eagerly:

'What happened at Marble Bridge, Your Honour? Half an hour ago the village headman brought the corpse of a woman to the tribunal. I ordered the coroner to conduct the autopsy. This is his report.'

He handed the paper he had been reading to the judge. Standing by the desk, Judge Dee glanced it through. The corpse was described as that of a young married woman, killed by a dagger-thrust that had penetrated into the heart. There were no bodily defects, but her shoulders were disfigured by old scars of undetermined origin. She had been in the third month of pregnancy.

Judge Dee gave the document back to Hoong, and seated himself in the large armchair behind his desk. He put the saddle-bag on the table, leaned back in his chair and asked:

'Did our headman bring in that fellow Sia Kwang, Tong Mai's friend?'

'No sir, he came an hour ago and told me that Sia hadn't returned yet. The old-clothes dealer, his landlord, said that it was no use waiting for Sia, for he keeps very irregular hours and often disappears for a day or two. The headman searched the attic Tong and Sia shared, then came back here. He left two constables there to watch the house till tomorrow morning, with orders to collar Sia as soon as he turns up.'

The sergeant cleared his throat and resumed:

'I had a long talk with Professor Ou-yang, sir. He doesn't share Dr Pien's and Mr Kou's high opinion of Tong. He told me that both Tong and Sia were clever enough, but dissolute youngsters, fond of wine and women, and not averse to shady financial deals. They were always very irregular in attending courses, and in recent months had hardly shown themselves in the temple school at all. The professor was not sorry about that, he said that those two had a bad influence on the other students. He was sorry for old Mr Tong, who was a learned, very cultured gentleman, he said. As to Sia Kwang, he thought that his parents lived in the capital. It seems they had disowned Sia because of his bad conduct.'

Judge Dee nodded. He sat up, took the saddle-bag and shook its contents out on the desk. Putting the two wrapped-up daggers aside, he untied the handkerchief and let the tortoise out. It crawled ahead, blinked solemnly at the candle, then withdrew into its shell. Sergeant Hoong stared at the small animal in speechless astonishment.

'If you let me have a large cup of hot tea, Hoong,' the judge said with a bleak smile, 'I'll tell you where and how I became acquainted with my small friend here.'

While the sergeant was busying himself over the tea-table in the corner, the judge got up and went, with the tortoise in his hand, to the back window. Leaning outside he placed the animal among the artificial rocks in the small, walled-in garden.

After he had resumed his seat, he gave Sergeant Hoong a detailed account of what had happened in the haunted house. He was interrupted only once, when the corporal of the south gate came in to report that neither he nor his colleagues at the other city gates had found a man with a fresh knife wound. When the corporal had taken his leave, Judge Dee told Hoong also about his interview with Kou Yuan-liang.

'So it's clear, Hoong,' he concluded, 'that the facts at our disposal now admit of two entirely different theories. I shall outline these for you, just for our general orientation, mind you, and mainly to map out a course for our investigation. Have a cup of tea, Hoong.'

The judge emptied his own cup, and resumed:

'In the first place, let us base ourselves on the assumption that Mr Kou told me the complete truth just now. In that case Tong Mai was poisoned by an unknown person who had learned about the planned sale of the pearl; he wanted to keep the appointment with the Amber Lady in Tong's place, and steal the gold and the pearl. He had not hesitated to murder Tong in order to achieve this purpose, and he didn't hesitate to kill Amber, either because she attacked him with a knife, or just to silence her. Less likely, but also possible, is that the man who kept the appointment with the Amber Lady had nothing to do with the poisoning of Tong Mai. But he did know about the impending transaction in the deserted house. When he learned that Tong had suddenly died, he then and there resolved to keep the appointment in Tong's place, in order to obtain the gold and the pearl. In that case Amber must have been killed by accident, for thieves and murderers belong to classes apart.'

57

Judge Dee paused. He caressed his side-whiskers for a while before he went on:

'My second theory is based on the assumption that Kou's statements were only partially true, and that he lied when he told me that he didn't know where the Amber Lady was going to meet Tong Mai. In that case Tong Mai and Amber were murdered on the instructions of Kou Yuan-liang.'

'How could that be possible, sir?' Sergeant Hoong exclaimed.

'Remember that Tong grew up together with Amber, Hoong! Tong was a likeable, handsome young man, and Amber an intelligent, attractive girl. Suppose that these two young people had become lovers? Unfortunately there are not a few householders who condone intimacy between their young sons and maids or slave-girls in the house, and old Mr Tong may have been one of those. If that was so, then it is quite possible that the lovers continued their liaison in secret, after Amber had entered Mr Kou's household.'

'That would have been black ingratitude on the part of Miss Amber!'

'It's often difficult to understand the actions of a woman in love, Hoong. Kou is a well-preserved, handsome man, but he is about twenty years older than she. And the autopsy showed that she was pregnant. Tong Mai might well be the father of her unborn child. Kou discovered that Amber was unfaithful to him; he kept his peace, waiting for an opportunity to take his revenge. That opportunity came when Amber told Kou about Tong's pearl. He realized that now he could kill the guilty pair, recover his gold, and obtain the coveted pearl—all at the same time. Kou had plenty of opportunities for poisoning Tong when he was entertaining the crews in the wine-house, in Marble Bridge Village. Having thus disposed of Tong, he had only to hire a ruffian to

58

keep the appointment in the deserted house, ordering him to kill the Amber Lady, take the gold bars, and find the pearl hidden by Tong in the pavilion.

'These are my two theories. I repeat, however, that all this is just guess-work. We must know a great deal more about the background of the persons concerned before we can take any definite action.'

The sergeant nodded slowly. Then he said worriedly:

'We'll have to do something about that pearl anyway, sir. Your unexpected arrival prevented the murderer from looking for it, it must still be in the pavilion. Shouldn't we go back to the deserted house now and make a search there?'

'No, that isn't necessary. Fortunately I ordered the village headman to post a strong guard there, just as a routine measure. Tomorrow morning we shall go there and make a search, in broad daylight. However, there's also another possibility, namely that Tong had been carrying the pearl on his person. Have we got his clothes here?'

The sergeant took a large sealed package from the wall-table. Judge Dee broke the seals and, together with Hoong, carefully searched the clothes. They felt all the seams, and the sergeant cut the soles of the shoes open. But they found nothing.

When Sergeant Hoong had packed up the clothes again, the judge silently drank another cup of tea. Then he said slowly:

'The fact that a theft from the Imperial Palace is connected with this murder case makes it an affair of the utmost gravity, Hoong. I find it rather difficult to assess Kou's personality. I would like to know a lot more about him. A pity that our best source of information, namely his First Lady, is useless because she is mentally deranged. Do you happen to know when and how she got that way, Hoong?'

'I have heard people talk about it, sir. It seems that it created quite a stir in this city, four years ago. Mrs Kou, Gold Lotus her personal name is, had gone out one night to visit a lady-friend living in the next street. But she never arrived there. She must have got an attack of brain-fever on the way, and lost her memory. It seems that she walked around aimlessly and apparently left the city by the east gate, passing the night roaming over the deserted fields. The next morning some peasants found her, lying in the grass, unconscious. She was dangerously ill for some weeks. When she had recovered, her mind was permanently deranged.'

The sergeant fell silent. He pensively fingered his thin grey moustache, then went on:

'When explaining your first theory, sir, you mentioned the possibility that Tong was murdered for a reason unconnected with the sale of the pearl. Now I remember that Tao Gan once told me that, although during the dragonboat races the betting of the common people involves only trifling amounts, wealthy traders and shopkeepers often bet considerable sums amongst each other. Tao Gan added that crooks sometimes practise all kinds of fraud and trickery with those large bets. Now it was generally assumed that Dr Pien's boat would win the race. If a crook knew beforehand that the drummer of Pien's boat would meet with an accident, he could make a small fortune by cornering bets. Perhaps it was such a crook who poisoned Tong Mai.'

'Yes,' Judge Dee said approvingly, 'that's another possibility we'll have to look into.'

There was a knock on the door. The headman entered and greeted the judge. He placed a soiled envelope on the desk and said:

'When I was searching the attic of those two students, Your Honour, I found this envelope in Sia's clothes-box.

60

Tong's box contained only a collection of worn-out clothes. Not a scrap of paper!'

'All right, headman, you may go.'

The judge tore the envelope open and took from it three folded pieces of paper. The first was a diploma from the Classical School stating that Sia Kwang had successfully passed his first examination, the second his permit to reside in Poo-yang. As the judge unfolded the third, he raised his eyebrows. He carefully smoothed the paper out on the desk. Pulling the candle closer he said: 'Look what we have got here, Hoong!'

The sergeant saw that it was a rough map of the area south of the city. Pointing with his finger, Judge Dee observed:

'Here we have the Mandrake Grove, and this rectangle here is the old Tong mansion. Only the east pavilion is marked on it. So Sia was also connected in some way or other with the sale of the pearl! Heavens, we must get hold of that fellow! And as soon as possible!'

'He's probably hanging about somewhere downtown, Your Honour. Our old friend Sheng Pa, the former self-styled boss of the underworld, will doubtless know where to find him!'

'Yes, we might ask him. Since I appointed him Head of the Beggars' Guild, Sheng Pa has shown himself very co-operative.'

'Unfortunately he is rather an elusive person, Your Honour. The only time he is sure to be home is late at night. For then the beggars assemble there to pay him his share of their earnings. I'd better go and see him right now, sir!'

'Out of the question! You must be dead tired. You go to bed, Hoong, that's where you go!'

'It'll mean a delay of one whole day, sir! Besides, I get along quite well with Sheng Pa; I have come to know the sly old devil's funny little ways. I think he likes me too—although he doesn't think much of your other three lieutenants. He once told me confidentially that he considers my friends Ma Joong and Chiao Tai a pair of vulgar bullies, and Tao Gan a mean crook!'

'That's a good one, coming from Sheng Pa!' the judge said with a smile. 'Well, if you insist, all right then. But go there in an official palankeen, and take four constables with you. Sheng Pa is living in an unsavoury neighbourhood.'

After Sergeant Hoong had left, Judge Dee drank another cup of tea. He was much more worried about the course of events than he had let it appear to his old adviser. The murder of a poor student had suddenly developed into a case of national importance, concerning a theft from the Imperial House. He would have to obtain quick results, for he could not postpone for long reporting to the higher authorities the news about the Emperor's pearl. Yet he had to tread warily. He heaved a deep sigh and rose. Deep in thought, he walked across the central courtyard to his own residence, in the back of the tribunal compound.

He had assumed that his wives would have gone to bed long before, and was planning to pass the night on the couch in his library. But, when the steward had opened the front door and was leading him inside, he heard peals of laughter coming from the brilliantly lit women's quarters. Seeing his master's astonished face, the greybeard explained quickly:

'The First Lady of General Bao and of the Hon'ble Wan, the retired judge, called earlier in the evening, sir. The ladies made together the customary offerings to the Queen of Heaven, then the First Lady invited them to stay for a game of cards. The First Lady instructed me to apprise her at once of Your Honour's return, so that she could dismiss her guests and attend upon Your Honour.'

'Just tell her to come to the ante-room for a moment.'

When his First Lady entered the small room, the judge noticed with pleasure how handsome she was looking in her favourite robe of violet brocade, embroidered with golden flowers. After she had made her bow she asked anxiously:

'I hope nothing untoward happened after the races?'

'There cropped up an affair that needed my immediate attention. I just wanted to tell you that you must on no account break up the party because of me. It was rather a tiresome evening, I feel like turning in now. I shall sleep in my library and the steward will wait upon me.'

When she was going to say good night, he suddenly asked:

'Did you find that missing domino, by the way?'

'No, I didn't. We agreed that it must have dropped overboard.'

'Impossible! Our table was standing in the centre of the platform. Where could that confounded domino have gone to?'

She raised her forefinger and said, half seriously, half in jest:

'In all the years we have been married I have never known you to fret about insignificant trifles. You won't start doing so now, I hope?'

'No, I won't!' Judge Dee replied with a faint smile. He nodded to her and went on to his library.

VIII

The wine-house where the Master of the Beggars' Guild had established his headquarters was located in the poor neighbourhood behind the Temple of the War God. The taproom was filled by a noisy crowd of beggars and vagabonds and smelled of stale sweat and cheap liquor. Sergeant Hoong had difficulty in elbowing his way towards the counter in the back.

Two ruffians clad in soiled robes stood there face to face, swearing loudly at each other. They were tall rogues, but the fat giant who stood leaning against the counter topped them by an inch or two. Clad in a threadbare black jacket and baggy, patched trousers, he had folded his arms, thick like masts, across the upper part of his enormous paunch. His large head was bare, the long locks were bound up with a dirty rag, and his full beard hung down in greasy strands. For a while he looked moodily from under his tufted eyebrows at the two quarrelling men. Suddenly he unfolded his arms, hitched up his trousers, and grabbed them by the scruff of the neck. Lifting them from the floor without any apparent effort, he smacked their heads together twice. When he let them drop on to the floor, Sergeant Hoong stepped up to him and said:

'I hate to disturb you, Sheng Pa. I see how fully occupied you are settling the city's administrative problems.' He cast a quick look at the two men, who were now sitting up dazedly rubbing their heads, and resumed: 'The fact is, however, that I have to see you rather urgently.'

The giant gave the sergeant a doubtful look.

'I am a sick man, Mister Sergeant,' he muttered, 'a very

64

'I AM A SICK MAN, MISTER SERGEANT'

sick man. But it shan't be said of me that I ignore the usages of polite society. Sit down over there with me, Mister Sergeant, and partake of some refreshment.'

When they were seated at the rickety corner-table with a bowl of reeking liquor in front of them, Sergeant Hoong said affably:

'I shan't take much of your valuable time, Sheng Pa. I only wanted to ask you for some information. About two vagrant students, fellows called Tong Mai and Sia Kwang. Scarface Sia, the latter is often called.'

Sheng Pa silently scratched his bare paunch. After a while he said ponderously:

'Vagrant young men of letters, eh? No sir, I wouldn't know nothing about those. Wouldn't like to know, either. Unlettered crooks being bad enough, it follows that lettered ones, learning many more dirty tricks from the books, are even worse. Don't wonder they get themselves into all sorts of trouble. I won't have any truck with them. Never.'

'One of them is dead. Had an accident, during the races.'

'May his soul rest in peace!' Sheng Pa said piously.

'Did you go to the races?'

'Me? No. I don't go in for betting. Can't afford it.'

'Come now, those few coppers?'

'Few coppers, you say? Let me tell you, Mister Sergeant, that lots of people lost a tidy bit on Number Nine! Including perhaps Pien the Leech, the owner. Very unfortunate for the doctor—*if* he lost, that is. My men told me that he has been a little short of cash, lately.' He looked studiously at his wine-cup, then added darkly: 'If there's big money involved, accidents will happen.'

'Who profited by the doctor's boat losing?'

Sheng Pa looked up and replied slowly:

'A tall question, Mister Sergeant, a very tall question! Those who corner bets are sly rascals, and no mistake! They

66

work through dozens of touts and middlemen. Who knows where the money finally goes to? Not me, sir!'

'Our judge would like to know, you see. It may be connected with a case he is investigating.'

'Involving a young man of letters, maybe.' The giant sadly shook his head, then repeated firmly: 'Very sorry I can't oblige.'

'I wouldn't be astonished,' Sergeant Hoong continued unabashed, 'if our judge handed out a good silver piece to the man who told him.'

Sheng Pa rolled up his large eyes.

'His Excellency the Judge!' he exclaimed ecstatically. 'Now, why didn't you say at once that it's him who wants to know! Have you ever known me to refuse co-operation with the high authorities? Pass by here tomorrow, Mister Sergeant, and maybe you'll find I'll be able to tell you a thing or two.'

Sergeant Hoong nodded and wanted to get up. But his host laid his large hand on his arm and asked reproachfully:

'What's the hurry, Mister Sergeant?' As Hoong reluctantly sat down again Sheng Pa went on earnestly: 'I like you, Mister Sergeant! It is my considered opinion that you are an honest man. The people of this city, and I mean the people that matter, mind you, hold you in high esteem.'

Hoong reflected sadly that this was a preliminary to a request for an advance on Judge Dee's reward. Feeling in his sleeve for money, he mumbled some self-deprecatory remarks. Sheng Pa interrupted him quickly:

'Don't let modesty obscure truth, sir! You are a man of wide and varied experience, and your years have bestowed upon you mature wisdom. Therefore I wish to entrust you with a delicate mission.' Seeing Hoong's blank face he added: 'No, you can't refuse an inoffensive old man a small favour! A man who is, moreover, grievously ill.'

'You don't look ill!' Hoong remarked. He had hardly recovered from his astonishment.

'It doesn't show, Mister Sergeant. It's in here, right inside my stomach.' There was a rumbling sound in his paunch, then he belched so loudly that the beggars stopped talking to give their boss an admiring look. 'You see? In my stomach. The most vital spot!'

'What's wrong with you?'

Sheng Pa leaned over to him and whispered hoarsely:

'It's a woman!'

The fat giant looked so unhappy that Sergeant Hoong held back the jocular remark that was on his lips. Instead he asked:

'Who is the lucky lady?'

'Lady is right!' Sheng Pa said with satisfaction. 'She was attached to the Imperial Court at one time. In the capital. She's a delicate creature. Sensitive. Therefore, she must be approached with the, ah . . . greatest circumspection.'

The sergeant gave his host a sharp look. A woman who had worked in the palace? Suddenly he sat up straight.

'Does the affair concern a pearl?' he asked eagerly.

'Wonderful! You always seem to know at once the right word, Mister Sergeant! A pearl, that's what she is! A pearl among women. Go to see her, sir, and put in a word for me. But with the greatest care, mind you! It wouldn't do to offend her maidenly modesty!'

Now the sergeant was completely at a loss. So it had nothing to do with the stolen pearl, after all. After some hesitation he asked:

'Do you want me to go to her as matchmaker, and propose on behalf of you?'

'Ho ho, not so fast!' Sheng Pa exclaimed aghast. 'Listen now! You being also a municipal officer, you'll understand

68

that in my position I couldn't afford a . . . er rebuttal, so to speak, isn't it? I have to keep to my principles, you see.'

'I don't understand this at all!' Hoong said crossly. 'What do you want me to do, after all?'

'I want you to go to her, and put in a word for me. That's all I want, sir! Put in a word for me. Just that, mind you. No more, no less!'

'I'll do that with pleasure. Where do I find her?'

'Go to the Temple of the War God, sir, and ask for the establishment of Miss Liang. Miss Violet Liang. Anybody about there will tell you.'

Sergeant Hoong rose.

'I am rather busy just now, Sheng Pa, but I'll go there as soon as I can find time. In a day or two, perhaps.'

'You'd better find time tomorrow morning, Mister Sergeant!' the giant said with a smug grin. 'It just came to my mind that those two fellows, Tong and Sia you called them if I remember correctly, visit Miss Liang's place. Rather often, I think. You ask Miss Violet Liang about them, Mister Sergeant! But gently, mind you. She is a delicate woman, she used to be attached to——'

'I know, to the Imperial Court. All right, Sheng Pa, I'll come here again some time tomorrow.'

IX

Early the next morning, just after breakfast, Sergeant Hoong found Judge Dee standing by the desk in his private office, feeding green leaves to the tortoise.

'It's remarkable how developed the senses of those animals are!' the judge remarked. 'To us these leaves have no smell at all, but look at this small fellow!'

He put a few salad leaves on the chair. The tortoise that was crawling over a book on the desk soon raised its head and made for the chair. Judge Dee put the leaves in front of him. When the tortoise had gobbled them up, he opened the window and put the small animal back into the rock-garden. Then he seated himself behind his desk and asked briskly:

'How did it fare last night, Hoong?'

The sergeant gave a detailed account of his meeting with Sheng Pa. When he had finished he added: 'Sheng Pa evidently had heard already that there was something wrong with Tong Mai's so-called accident. And also rumours about the bets having been manipulated. He even suggested that, since Dr Pien is short of money, he might have cornered the bets and profited by his own boat losing the race.'

The judge raised his eyebrows.

'He did, did he?' He tugged at his moustache. 'That puts the doctor in a very curious light. I had the impression that he's looked upon here as a well-to-do, worthy citizen, of unquestioned integrity. Looks quite a dignified fellow too, with that solemn, pale face and that jet-black moustache. I admit, however, that he was rather keen to have Tong's death recorded as due to heart failure. Did you ever hear anything against him, Hoong?'

'No sir. He is generally considered one of the best physicians in this town. It's a pity that Sheng Pa expresses himself so darkly. I wager that he knows more about Tong Mai and Sia Kwang than he wants to admit. But he'd rather die than make a straightforward statement!'

Judge Dee nodded.

'It's clear,' he said, 'that he prefers us to hear the information about Tong and Sia directly from the woman he mentioned. We shall go and see her this morning. Hasn't Sia come back yet to his lodging? I'd like to meet him first of all, then hear what Sheng Pa's girl-friend has to say about him and Tong Mai.'

'Unfortunately Sia hasn't come back to his lodging, sir. The headman told me that just now one of the constables who was watching Sia's place came back and reported that Sia hasn't turned up.' Hoong paused. After a while he resumed, rather diffidently: 'Speaking about Sheng Pa's girl-friend, Your Honour, it might be possible that the old scoundrel somehow or other has got the wind of the sale of the pearl, and wanted to give me to understand that the woman knows something about that affair. What else could he have meant by stressing so much that she had been attached to the Imperial Palace—which is of course the purest nonsense!'

The judge shrugged his shoulders.

'Remember that there are thousands of women employed in the palace, Hoong. Including charwomen and scullery maids. As to the Emperor's pearl, you can get that fabulous treasure out of your head! For I have come to the conclusion that the whole story is a hoax, Hoong! A fairy-tale, from beginning to end!'

The astonished sergeant opened his mouth to say something, but the judge went on quickly:

'It was a hoax, Hoong. And, what is more, I am convinced

that Kou knew it! I didn't sleep too well, I couldn't get that tale about the pearl out of my head. I went over again and again the story of how it disappeared, and how Tong Mai got hold of it. And came to the conclusion that the pearl doesn't exist. Listen, carefully! As I explained to you last night, it is more than probable that Tong Mai and Amber had a liaison. A couple of months ago Amber informs her lover that she is pregnant, and that he is the father. They realize that they can't keep the affair secret any longer, and they decide to flee together. But how to get the money? Then the two of them concoct the story of the Emperor's pearl. Amber informs her husband that Tong has hidden the pearl in a safe place, and she offers to go there and conclude the transaction. The lovers will meet in the pavilion, and elope together, with the ten gold bars. A clever plan! However, they did not know that Kou had found out their secret relations already, and was only waiting for a chance to take his revenge. Kou would have been a fool if he hadn't figured out that the safe place known to both Tong and Amber referred to the deserted villa. Kou feigns to believe Amber's story. He poisons Tong, and hires a ruffian to kill Amber in the pavilion and bring the gold back to him. What do you think about that, Hoong?'

The sergeant looked doubtful. He replied slowly:

'Last night I refrained from further comment on Your Honour's theory about Mr Kou's guilt, because we were then just surveying various possibilities. But now that a definite case against Kou is being formulated, sir, I must confess that I can't see a quiet gentleman of refined taste like Mr Kou perpetrating such a foul crime. And there are so many other possibilities to be considered. Just now we discussed Dr Pien and his——'

'Jealousy can make even a quiet man commit violent deeds!' Judge Dee interrupted. 'Be that as it may, we'll go to the deserted villa and have a second look at the pavilion. I am convinced that the pearl is non-existent, but I'd like to see the scene of the murder in broad daylight. And an early-morning ride will do us good! If, upon returning to the city, we find that Sia Kwang hasn't shown up yet, we'll go straight to Sheng Pa's girl-friend, and see whether she can direct us to that elusive fellow. I must absolutely have a talk with him before I open the morning session of the tribunal.'

As Judge Dee rose, his eye fell on the book the tortoise had been crawling on.

'Oh yes,' he resumed, 'I forget to tell you! I slept badly as I told you, and I woke up an hour or so before daybreak. I did a bit of reading in an interesting book I borrowed a few days ago from the chancery library.'

He took the volume, opened it on the place indicated by a book-marker, and went on:

'This is a collection of notes on this district, privately published about fifty years ago by a former magistrate here who took a great interest in the past history of the region. One day he made a trip to the ruined temple of the River Goddess in the Mandrake Grove. In his time there still was a passable road leading up to it. This is what he says:

"The outer wall and the gatehouse have been damaged considerably by the earthquake, but the main hall and the famous statue of the goddess still stand. The statue represents a woman, more than ten feet high, standing erect on a pedestal, all carved out of one block of marble. The square altar in front of the statue has been cut from one and the same block. A remarkable work of art indeed!"'

Judge Dee brought the book closer to his eyes and said:

'Here a former reader wrote a note in the margin, in red ink. It says:

"My esteemed colleague is wrong. I visited the temple ten years later, and found that the altar is in fact made of a separate block of marble. I had the cement in between pedestal and altar removed, because I had heard that formerly the priests had made a cache in the altar, for storing the golden ritual vessels; I thought that those valuable objects ought to be removed to a safe place, for instance to the treasury of the Ministry of Rites. But I failed to discover any sign of the altar being hollow. Twan, Magistrate of Poo-yang."

'Twan was a conscientious official,' Judge Dee remarked. 'I now go on with the printed text:

"There is a golden ring with a magnificent large ruby on the forefinger of the statue's left hand. The village headman told me that this ruby is supposed to be the Evil Eye, and that hence no one would ever dare to steal it. The square altar has a hole in each upper corner, used for fastening the ropes of the young men who were sacrificed there yearly on the fifth of the fifth month, having been chosen by drawing lots. The high priest cut the victim's veins with a jade knife, then sprinkled his blood all over the statue. Thereafter the body was carried in a festive procession to the river-bank and solemnly committed to the waves. A truly barbarous custom, fortunately discontinued some years ago on the orders of our wise Government. The statue is reputedly always wet, and I found its smooth surface indeed covered with moisture, but whether this phenomenon is to be ascribed to dew or to some supernatural cause, I leave to the learned reader to

74

decide. I was greatly struck by the uncanny atmosphere of that strange place, and left sooner than I had intended, taking one of the dated bricks of the crumbling wall with me, for my reference."

'That is all. Curious affair!' Judge Dee put the book on the desk and motioned Sergeant Hoong to follow him outside. In the courtyard he ordered the headman to bring two horses from the stables.

They left the city by the south gate. A cool morning mist was hanging over the Canal, so that they had a pleasant ride to Marble Bridge.

There they first went to see the village headman. He told the judge that the militia had come back towards daybreak, after a rather uncomfortable night. One fellow maintained he had heard ghostly voices whisper in the Mandrake Grove, another that he had seen a white shape flutter about among the trees. The men had sat up the entire night, huddled together in the walled-in garden in front of the pavilion. The headman added that he had sealed the door of the pavilion after he had removed the dead body of the Amber Lady.

Judge Dee nodded his approval, and they rode on. Having passed the market, where the vendors were busy putting up their stalls, they took the road to the forest. Arrived at the old pine-tree that marked the entrance to the Tong property, Judge Dee dismounted and fastened the reins to its gnarled trunk. The sergeant followed his example. They went on ahead on foot.

The judge found that in broad daylight the walk to the deserted villa did not take very long. Soon they saw the weather-beaten gatehouse and the ivy-overgrown walls.

When Judge Dee was passing underneath the arched doorway leading to the walled-in garden, he suddenly halted and laid his hand on Hoong's arm. A tall, broad-shouldered man clad in a long black robe and wearing a black gauze cap was standing in front of the pavilion, with his back towards them. The door of the pavilion stood ajar, the torn strip of paper with which it had been sealed fluttered in the morning breeze.

'Hey there!' Judge Dee called out. 'Who are you and what are you doing here?'

The man in black turned round and silently looked the newcomers up and down with his lidded eyes. He had a placid, round face with a short moustache and a carefully trimmed ringbeard. When he had completed his leisurely scrutiny he spoke in a cultured voice:

'That abrupt address would ordinarily provoke an equally abrupt retort. Since, however, your carriage and manner suggest authority, I shall limit myself to the observation that it is I who should ask the same questions. For you are trespassing on my property.'

The judge did not waste words. He said sharply:

'I am the magistrate of this district, conducting an official investigation. Answer my questions!'

The other made a low bow, then replied courteously:

'I have the honour to report that my name is Kwang Min. I am a retail drug merchant, from the capital. I purchased this property four years ago, from the former owner, Mr Tong I-kwan.'

'Strange things have happened here. I want proof of your identity.'

The man in black made another low bow, then took from his sleeve two papers, which he presented to the judge. The first was an identity document issued by the metropolitan governor, the second a detailed map of the entire Tong property, issued four years previously by the tribunal of

76

Poo-yang, to Mr Kwang Min, the new owner. Giving the papers back, Judge Dee said:

'All right. Now tell me why you broke the official seal attached to the door of the pavilion over there. That's a criminal offence, you know!'

'I did not!' Kwang said indignantly. 'I found the door standing ajar.'

'Why did you come here on this unusual hour?'

'If Your Honour doesn't object to a rather long story, I——'

'I do object. So be brief!'

'The essential facts,' Mr Kwang resumed unperturbed, 'may be summed up as follows. Four years ago my customer Dr Pien Kia informed me by letter that this property could be purchased cheap, and advised me to buy, since the adjoining forest contained a large number of mandrake plants. My firm is always keen to acquire such plots, for, as Your Honour is doubtless aware, the roots of the mandrake figure largely in the drug business. I consequently bought the property. Since, however, my firm was well supplied with the roots at that time, it was only two years later that I decided to send one of my surveyors to have a look. Then Dr Pien wrote me that there was a drought in this region, and warned me that the local people might resent my surveyor exploring the wood over there, which seems to be dedicated to the River Goddess. She is supposed to——'

'I know, I know,' Judge Dee interrupted him impatiently. 'Get on with your story!'

'I obey Your Honour's command. During the next two years I was fully occupied by other matters, it was only yesterday morning, when my barge had arrived at Marble Bridge, that I remembered I possessed a plot of land near by, and——'

'What brought you to Marble Bridge? A pleasure trip?'

'On the contrary,' Kwang replied stiffly, 'it was urgent business, connected with the affairs of my branch-office, further up the Canal. Three days ago I chartered a canal-junk, together with my friend and colleague Mr Sun, intending to proceed north with the least possible delay. However, when our boatmen heard on arrival that at night a dragon-boat race would be held here on grand scale, the lazy rascals insisted on staying over here the night. Thinking that I might as well put this enforced delay to some good use, I sent a message to Dr Pien asking him to come to Marble Bridge at noon, and show me over the former Tong property. He replied that he was fully occupied with the preparations for the races, but that he would call on me late in the afternoon. He came for tea to my junk, and we agreed to meet here in the deserted house today, shortly after daybreak. I chose the early hour because it was—and still is, by Your Honour's leave—my intention to set sail again as soon as possible. Now I am waiting here for Dr Pien. I am pleased that a lucky chance brought Your Honour here also, for last night modesty prevented me from presenting myself.'

As he saw Judge Dee's questioning look, Mr Kwang continued with the same bland expression:

'Last night Dr Pien kindly took me to a wine-house in Marble Bridge Village where he was entertaining the crews and, thereafter, down the Canal to the locality of the finish. Then Dr Pien had to busy himself about the races. While I was walking around aimlessly on the river-bank, a passer-by pointed out Your Honour's barge to me, and I made bold to go on board. For I have many business relations in Poo-yang, and I felt I ought to pay my respects to its magistrate. There was no one on the lower deck to announce me, and when I went up I saw Your Honour and his ladies standing at the railing, enjoying the scenery. Not wishing to intrude on what evidently was a family gathering, I withdrew. I

78

met the steward on the lower deck, and told him not to bother. I feel, however, that I ought to mention this, in order to prove that I am not lacking in——'

'Quite. Very kind of you Mr Kwang.' Judge Dee gave him a steady look. So this was the mysterious visitor his steward had spoken about. He asked: 'Did your colleague, Mr Sun, accompany you?'

'No sir. Since he was indisposed, he retired early to his cabin. As to me, I saw the finish of the races, then hired a horse and rode back to Marble Bridge. None of my boatmen had returned yet, the dissolute loafers, so I made myself a cup of tea and retired also.'

'All right, thank you, Mr Kwang. Now tell me, why did you have the pavilion over there repaired?'

Mr Kwang raised his thin eyebrows in polite astonishment.

'Repaired? Dismantled you mean for sure, sir!'

Judge Dee went past him and up the steps, followed by Sergeant Hoong and Kwang. Standing just inside the door, he surveyed the room with an incredulous stare. Large patches of the plaster had been torn from the walls, showing the red bricks underneath. Part of the ceiling had been taken down, floor-tiles removed, even the bamboo legs of the couch had been split open.

'What's going on here?' an astonished voice spoke up behind them.

Judge Dee turned round. He said sourly:

'Unauthorized persons have made mischief here, Dr Pien. We are just taking stock of the damage.'

'I was under the impression, doctor.' Kwang addressed him coldly, 'that you had agreed in writing to keep an eye on my property.'

'I sent a man up here only a month ago, Mr Kwang,' Dr Pien replied with a vexed expression. 'He reported that everything was in order. And he knew this place inside out. It was Tong Mai, the son of the former owner. I can't understand this at all, I——'

'I'll be back presently,' Judge Dee interrupted. He motioned the sergeant to follow him.

As they were crossing the garden the judge said in a low voice:

'The murderer came back very early this morning, just when the militia had left. He must have believed the story about the Emperor's pearl, and came to look for it. Let's see whether he visited the main building too.' He angrily slapped at a few bluebottles that buzzed round his head.

A quick tour through the deserted halls proved that nothing had been disturbed there. The judge saw only his own footprints on the dust-covered floor. When they were walking back to the pavilion the sergeant remarked:

'The pavilion was searched completely. That would seem to indicate that the murderer did not find what he came for.'

Judge Dee nodded. He again hit out at a swarm of bluebottles. 'Confound those insects! Look, Hoong, it was here, on top of this wall, that I saw that small tortoise.' Putting his hands on the low wall he went on: 'It was crawling along under a——'

Suddenly he broke off. He leaned forward over the wall and looked down on the other side. Hoong joined him. He uttered a smothered oath.

The body of a man dressed in a blue jacket and trousers was lying among the weeds in the shallow ditch at the foot of the wall. Uncounted bluebottles were crawling over the top of his skull, which was a mass of clotted blood.

The judge turned round and rushed inside the pavilion. Dr Pien and Mr Kwang stood in a corner, deep in conversation. Judge Dee stepped up to them and asked Kwang casually:

THE JUDGE AND HOONG MAKE A DISCOVERY

'How long had you been here when I arrived, Mr Kwang?'

'I came here only a few moments before Your Honour,' Kwang answered. 'I hadn't even inspected the main building. I came first to the garden here, to have a look at the Mandrake Grove beyond the wall, because——'

'Come along, both of you!' barked the judge.

As soon as Kwang had looked over the wall he turned away, retched and was violently sick.

'That's Sia Kwang, sir!' Dr Pien exclaimed. 'You can see the scar on his left cheek!'

Judge Dee tucked up his robe, climbed on the wall and let himself down on the other side. Dr Pien and Sergeant Hoong scrambled over the wall after him.

Squatting by the dead man's side, the judge scrutinized the bloodstained hair. Then he looked round among the weeds in the ditch. He picked up a brick and handed it to Hoong, saying:

'The top of his skull was bashed in from behind with this brick. You can still see the blood, on its side here.' Rising, he added: 'Help me to search the shrubbery, there may be other clues.'

'This looks like a carpenter's tool box, sir!' the sergeant exclaimed. He showed the judge the scarred, oblong box he had found under a shrub. On a sign from Judge Dee Hoong undid the leather straps. The box contained two saw-blades, a hammer, and a few chisels.

'Take that along too,' the judge said. And, to Dr Pien: 'Help me to take off his jacket!'

After they had stripped the dead man's muscular torso they saw that a rag was wound tightly round the left upper-arm. Dr Pien loosened it and examined the deep cut.

'The wound was inflicted very recently, sir,' he remarked. 'With a thin, sharp knife, I'd say. The body is still warm,

82

he must have been killed only half an hour ago or so!'

Judge Dee said nothing. He searched the sleeves, but they were empty. Neither was anything tucked among the folds of the sash round the man's waist, not even a handkerchief. The judge said curtly:

'We are through here. Our coroner shall do the rest.'

X

When the three men had climbed back into the garden again, Judge Dee cut short Kwang Min's excited questions and said to Hoong:

'Ride to the market and fetch the village headman and a dozen or so local militia.'

He began to pace the garden, from time to time angrily shaking his sleeves. Dr Pien took Mr Kwang apart and started a whispered conversation.

Sergeant Hoong came back in a remarkably short time. He brought a flustered headman and a group of frightened-looking youngsters, armed with long bamboo sticks.

Judge Dee ordered the village headman to have the corpse put on a stretcher and brought to the tribunal. His men were to stay and guard the house till the constables would come to take over. Seeing their unhappy faces, he snapped at them:

'It's broad daylight now, isn't it? There's nothing to be afraid of!' He added to Pien and Kwang: 'We'll return to the village together. You two may borrow horses from the militia here.'

When the cavalcade had arrived in Marble Bridge Village, Judge Dee told Mr Kwang to take them to his junk.

It proved to be quite a big barge that took up most of the space afforded by the quay beyond the bridge. Four haggard-looking boatmen were unrolling the sail of bamboo-matting. The judge told Kwang and the two others to wait on the jetty, and walked over the narrow plank that served as gangway to the ship. Standing on the foredeck he shouted for the captain. After a long wait a tousled head rose up from the hatch. The captain stepped on deck, hitched up his trousers and stared at the judge with bleary, bloodshot eyes. Evidently he and his crew had a rather heavy night behind them.

'Take me to Mr Sun!' Judge Dee ordered.

The captain shambled to the raised stern, consisting of a double cabin. After repeated knocking on the narrow door, the window by its side was pushed open. A thin man with a scraggy neck and an aggressive short beard leaned out. A white cloth was wound tightly round his head.

'Do you have to make that awful noise?' he asked crossly. 'I am suffering from a splitting headache. I shouldn't be disturbed!'

'I am the magistrate. No, stay where you are! I only want to ask you how you passed last evening, Mr Sun.'

'In bed, sir. Didn't even have one bite for dinner. These attacks bother me regularly, you know. Confounded nuisance.' He put his elbows on the sill and went on: 'Not that I have no warning, though. The first sign is a feverish feeling, and complete lack of appetite. It is followed by a slight sickness, accompanied by a sour taste in my mouth, and then——'

'Most distressing. Did Mr Kwang come to see you?'

'He did. He looked in before dinner to tell me he was off to the boat races, with a friend of his. Didn't hear him come back. But you'll doubtless find him in his cabin, next to mine here. Was there an accident?'

'I am looking for witnesses. A man was murdered.'

Mr Sun gave the slovenly captain a baleful look.

'Evidently the victim wasn't our captain!' he remarked with a sigh. 'A great pity. I never was on a worse-run boat!'

The captain began to mutter indignantly, but the judge turned to him and snapped: 'You'll sail this boat down to the landing-stage near the west gate of the city, and keep it there until further notice!' And, to Mr Sun: 'I am afraid you'll have to stay here for a day or two, Mr. Sun. You might utilize the delay for consulting a doctor. I wish you a speedy recovery.'

Mr Sun started to protest that he was in a great hurry to travel on, but Judge Dee turned his back on him and went on land.

'You are an important witness,' he told Mr Kwang. 'Therefore you'll have to break your journey here. I told the captain to bring the junk to the landing-stage, you can either stay on board or take a room in a hostel, as you like. But report your address to the tribunal at once, so that I can summon you when I need you.' Kwang frowned and was going to say something, but the judge continued in a crisp voice to Pien: 'I'll be needing you too, doctor. You are not to leave the city for the time being. Goodbye.'

He jumped on his horse and rode off, together with Sergeant Hoong. When they were riding along the highway the sun had risen higher and was scorching them with its pitiless rays.

'We should have taken straw hats along!' Judge Dee muttered.

'It's bound to grow hotter still, sir! Not a breeze is stirring, and I don't like those small black clouds gathering over there. We may be in for a thunderstorm, later in the day.'

The judge made no comment. They rode on in silence. When the south gate came into sight Judge Dee suddenly burst out:

'That's the third murder in two days! And of Sia Kwang, the only man who could have shed some light on this baffling business!' Then he went on in a calmer voice: 'I'll tell you frankly that I am worried, Hoong. There's a dangerous, completely ruthless criminal on the loose in our town.'

The corporal of the guard had seen them approaching. Now he stood stiffly at attention in front of the guardhouse, inside the gate. Through the window came a rattling sound. Two soldiers were sorting out bamboo markers on the high table. Judge Dee halted his horse, bent down from the saddle and looked through the window. After a while he righted himself, and pensively let his riding-whip swing to and fro. He had a vague feeling that those rattling markers ought to remind him of something that was in the back of his mind. But the connection was just out of his reach. He knitted his eyebrows.

The corporal looked at him, astonished. He said awkwardly:

'It is, ah . . . a rather hot day, Excellency.'

Deep in thought, Judge Dee had not heard him. Suddenly he smiled broadly. Turning to Hoong on the horse behind him, he exclaimed:

'Holy Heaven, that must be it, of course!' Then he said briskly to the corporal: 'Let those two men of yours arrange all those markers according to their numbers. If they should find two that bear the same number, send those to the tribunal at once!'

He urged on his horse.

Hoong wanted to ask the judge what was wrong with the markers, but Judge Dee said quickly:

'I'll go to see Sheng Pa's girl-friend myself. You go to the Kou mansion and find out from the servants whether Kou went out this morning. I don't care whether you bully or bribe, as long as you get that information!'

'What about the morning session of the tribunal, sir?' the sergeant asked worriedly. 'The news of the Amber Lady's murder will have spread throughout the city now, and soon the people will know about Sia Kwang's death too. If we don't issue some sort of official statement, tongues

87

will begin to wag and all kinds of fantastic stories will be told in the tea houses ! '

Judge Dee pushed his cap back from his perspiring brow.

'You are right of course, Hoong ! Let it be announced that there'll be no morning session today, but that the court will convene at noon. I'll then just make known the bare facts and add a non-committal statement about the investigation being in progress. Let's exchange our caps. I have no idea who or what that Miss Liang is, so that I had better go there incognito.'

After he had put on Hoong's small skull-cap, they parted. Judge Dee rode in the direction of the Temple of the War God. Wearing that cap and covered with dust and perspiration as he was, he hoped that he would not be recognized.

XI

The street urchin whom he asked after Miss Liang's house did not give him a second look. He silently pointed with a dirty forefinger at a large wooden barrack, near the corner of the street.

When Judge Dee had dismounted and was fastening the bridle of his horse to the ring in the wall, his eye fell on the red-lacquered signboard hanging next to the door. It was inscribed with four black letters in cursive writing that read *Wu-te Tao-chang*, 'Training Hall of Martial Virtue'. The large square seal at the top indicated that the inscription had been written by one of the Imperial Princes. Doubtfully shaking his head he went inside.

It was fairly cool in the dim, spacious hall. In the centre a thick reed mat had been spread out on the floor. Six hefty men, stripped to the waist, were practising wrestling-grips there in pairs. Farther on two dishevelled ruffians were fencing with bamboo sticks. Half a dozen men were sitting on the wooden bench against the side wall, intently following the proceedings. No one paid any attention to the newcomer.

One of the fencers got hit on his hand. He let his stick drop and began to curse volubly.

'Mind your language, Mister Mo, if you please!' a grating voice resounded from the back of the hall.

The fencer looked round with a frightened face.

'Yes Miss Liang!' he said meekly. 'Sorry Miss Liang!'

He blew on his sore fingers, picked up his stick, and the fencing went on.

Judge Dee walked round the wrestlers and up to the

counter. Then he stood stock-still. He stared with unbeliev-
ing eyes at the colossal woman reclining in the armchair
there. This mountain of flesh was clad in a short-sleeved
jacket and wide trousers of rough brown cotton, as worn by
professional wrestlers. One red sash was wound tightly round
her barrel-like torso under her ample bosom, and a second
round her waist, supported her paunch. Raising her round,
expressionless face up to the judge, she asked in a rasping
voice:

'What do you want, stranger?'

Taking hold of himself, the judge spoke gruffly:

'My name is Jen, I am a boxing-master from the capital.
I have to stay here for a few weeks, and Mr Sheng Pa
directed me here, for advice about getting a few pupils. To
keep my rice-bowl filled, you see?'

Miss Liang did not reply at once. She raised her heavy
right arm and patted her hair, combed straight back over
her bullet-like head and gathered in a small bun in her
neck. She was looking steadily at the judge all the while.
Suddenly she said:

'Let me feel your hand!'

His hand was buried in her ham-like, calloused fist. He
was a strong man, but he winced involuntarily. He had to
summon all his strength to counter the pressure of the vice-
like grip. Suddenly she let go.

'All right,' she said. 'So you are a boxing-master. They
come with beard and whiskers nowadays, it seems.' She rose
with surprising agility, strode round the counter and
filled two rice-bowls from a stone wine-jar. 'Have a drink,
colleague!' she said casually.

He saw that she was as tall as himself. Her head seemed
to grow directly from her broad, round shoulders. While
sipping the rather good wine he asked curiously:

'Where did you learn the trade?'

'Far up north. I led a troupe of Mongolian women wrestlers, you know. A few years ago, when we came to the capital for a demonstration, the Third Prince engaged us for the Palace. The whole Court, gentlemen and ladies, used to turn out to see our naked wrestling bouts. I say naked, but we did wear a small brocade apron in front, mind you! We are modest girls.' She emptied her bowl in one draught, spat on the floor and went on: 'Last year the Minister of Rites reported to the Throne that our wrestling was indecent. Indecent my foot! You know who was behind it? It was those Court ladies! They were jealous, couldn't bear that their men saw what it takes to make a real woman, for once! Those skinny, measly bits of skirt! Bah, if Merciful Heaven hadn't given them a nose, you couldn't tell their front from their behind. Anyway, the Throne ordered the Prince to dismiss us.'

'Where are the other women of your troupe?'

'Went back to our country. I stayed. I like China. The Third Prince gave me a whole gold bar when I left. "When you get married, Violet, don't forget to let me know!" His Highness said. "I'll present the groom with a step-ladder, all of silver, for he'll be needing that for ascending you!" He was fond of his little jokes, His Highness was!' She shook her large head with a reminiscent smile.

Judge Dee knew that she was not boasting. Ministers of State could approach the Princes only on their bended knees, but those exalted persons were wont to treat the acrobats and jugglers they patronized as their equals.

'Sport is the only thing I am interested in,' Miss Liang resumed, 'so I started this training-hall. I charge the men only for what they drink, the instruction is free. Some of those fellows show promise.'

'I heard that two are especially good. Couple of vagrant students by the name of Tong and Sia, I think.'

'You are behind the time, my friend! Tong is dead. Good riddance to bad rubbish.'

'Why? I was told that Tong was an able boxer and a likeable fellow.'

'He wasn't too bad, as a boxer, that is. As to likeable . . .' She turned round and bellowed: 'Rose!'

A thin girl of about sixteen appeared from behind the door curtain in the back wall. She was drying a saucer with a rag.

'Leave that dish alone, put your nose to the wall and show your backside!' Miss Liang ordered.

The girl obediently turned her back to them. She loosened the upper part of her robe and let her arms slip out of the sleeves. Her skinny back was covered with white scars. As she was about to loosen her sash, Miss Liang growled: 'That'll do! Dress up and go on with the dishes.'

'Did Tong Mai do that?' Judge Dee asked.

'Not exactly. But Tong was around here a lot, till a few weeks ago. The foolish wench took a liking to him and let him take her out one night. He brings her to a place somewhere in the north quarter. In the dark the only thing she can see is that it's rather a big house. He takes her to a dark room. She can't see who is there, but before she knows what is happening she is stripped, fixed face down to a couch and beaten up. As you saw. Later Tong comes back, unties her, and brings her back to this street. Gives her a silver piece, tells her to keep her mouth shut and disappears. Stupid wench tells me only a couple of days ago, when I happen to walk in on her when she is bathing and see the welts. Pity Tong is dead, I had planned to do the same to him, only more thoroughly. Well, the gallivanting jade got a good lesson, anyway.'

'Was she raped too?'

'No, she's still a virgin—for the time being. Else I would

92

have reported the affair to the tribunal, of course. I know my duties. But the wench went of her own free will, and accepted payment for it. So what could I do?'

'Did Tong often procure girls for degenerate lechers?'

'Apparently. But only for one. Same fellow as he hunted out curios for, I believe. Tong got into trouble with that kind patron, recently. Tong was an ambitious scoundrel, wanted too much money, perhaps. But I think that his friend Sia, that stupid bastard, took over the good work.'

'Sia did you say? Why do you think that?'

'Sia is not as clever as Tong, not by a long way. Yesterday morning he comes in here, he's had a few drinks, which isn't anything unusual. What is unusual is that he pays his drinking debt to me. I ask: "Have you bumped into the Money Tree?" "Not yet," he says, "but tonight I am going to get a lot of money. I promised to put a chicken in a coop for a fellow." "Better be careful that you don't land up in a coop yourself!" I say. "Don't worry!" he says with his toothy grin. "It's a lonely place, no one will hear the cackling! And Tong says that the fellow always pays on the dot!" I lay my hand on his shoulder, friendly-like, and I say: "Out you go, Sia my boy, and let me never see your ugly scarred mug again!" He sails across the hall against the doorpost over there. When he has come to, he scrambles up and from the door shouts rude things at me. Then I nail his sleeve to the post, like this.'

While she was speaking a long knife had suddenly appeared in her hand. Now it flew across the hall and landed in the doorpost with a dull thud. There was a hush in the hall. The two fencers went to the door. With difficulty they pulled the quivering knife from the wood and brought it back to Miss Liang with respectful bows. She remarked with a complacent grin:

'If I get nervous, I am liable to start throwing things about!'

'If you aren't careful, you might get into trouble some day!' Judge Dee warned her.

'Me? I am afraid of nobody! Not even of the authorities. When I left the Palace, His Highness gave me a paper with a seal on it as large as your head. It says that I still belong to the Imperial Household, and that I can be judged by the Palace Tribunal only. Well, you asked about Tong and Sia. Now you know. Anything else I can do for you, Mister Magistrate?' Seeing Judge Dee's startled look, she scoffed: 'You didn't think you could fool a woman who has been rubbing shoulders with high officials for years, did you now? I know one when I see him! Else I wouldn't have been blabbing to you as I did, would I? Mark my words, Magistrate, Tong was no good and Sia is no good.'

'For Sia you can use the past tense too, Miss Liang. This morning he was killed, most probably by the same scoundrel who used to employ him. Do you know who he is?'

'No sir, I don't. I asked Rose, but the wench hasn't got the faintest idea. She was fixed to that couch face-down, remember, and he never said a word. Only laughed. If I had known who he was, you could have sent your constables to gather up what I had left of him. I object to those kind of people.'

'Well, you gave me most useful information. By the way, Sheng Pa asked me to put in a good word for him with you.'

Suddenly her broad face lit up.

'He did, did he?' she said coyly. Then she frowned and asked sternly: 'Does he intend to send me a middleman, charged with offering a formal proposal?'

'Well, not exactly. He only asked——'

'To put in a word for him, eh? The stubborn bastard! He has been sending all kinds of fellows over here of late, to

94

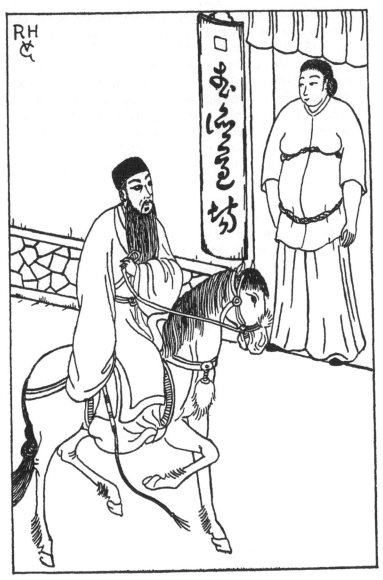

JUDGE DEE TAKES LEAVE OF MISS LIANG

put in a word for him! Well, I won't say yes or no, he'll have to take his chance. He's a fine, upstanding man, Sheng Pa is, I'll admit that. But I have my principles.'

'The trouble is that he seems to have his principles too,' Judge Dee observed. 'But I can tell you that he has a steady income, and that I find him a useful and dependable fellow— in his own peculiar way.' Thinking that he had done enough for redeeming Sergeant Hoong's promise, he set down his bowl and said: 'Thanks very much. I'll be on my way now.'

She saw him to the door. In passing she said to a squat fellow who was sitting on the bench against the side wall:

'We'll now go through those strangleholds once more, Mister Ko, if you please.'

The man went pale under his tan, but he rose obediently.

The street outside was as hot as an oven. Judge Dee quickly mounted his horse, nodded at Miss Liang, who was standing at the door, and rode off.

XII

The judge guided his horse in a western direction. Miss Liang's information had introduced an entirely new element into the murder cases. He had therefore decided to make one more call before going back to the tribunal.

Arrived at the Temple of Confucius, he halted in front of a neatly plastered, two-storied building across the street. The windows of the ground floor were provided with iron bars, those of the second floor had a row of long spikes all along the sill to prevent thieves from climbing up there. A discreet small signboard over the door bore the name of the shop: 'Treasurehouse of Antiquity'. The judge dismounted and fastened the reins to a stone post, where an awning provided shade for his horse.

The young shop-assistant came to meet him with a broad smile.

'Mr Yang has just come back, sir! He rode out to a farm where they had dug up an old inscribed stone. He is now in his study upstairs.'

He led Judge Dee along the cupboards crammed with smaller and larger antiques to the staircase at the back.

The spacious room upstairs was artificially cooled by two copper basins on the floor, piled with iceblocks. A diffuse light filtered through the two high windows, covered by paper screens. Faded scroll paintings hung on the wall space in between, and against the side wall stood a rack piled with dog-eared books.

The huge curio-dealer was sitting at a table of polished ebony. Leaning back in his armchair, he was examining a slender vase of red porcelain which he held in his large hands. When his assistant announced the arrival of the magistrate, Yang carefully set the vase down on the table, then quickly got up. He made a low bow, pulled up another armchair to the table and said in his booming voice:

'Your Honour doubtless wants to see that fine painting I mentioned last night! It'll be found worth an inspection, I trust! But let me first offer you a cup of tea, sir!'

Judge Dee sat down and accepted a round silk fan from the assistant.

'I shall be grateful for a cup of tea, Mr Yang,' he said, fanning himself, 'but the painting will have to wait till some other time. I dropped in here in order to obtain some information. Confidentially.'

The curio-dealer motioned his assistant to leave them alone. He himself poured out the tea, then he sat back in his chair, looking expectantly at his visitor with his shrewd eyes.

'I am faced with no less than three murders, Mr Yang,' the judge began. 'You know about Tong Mai and the Amber Lady, and you will probably have heard already that this morning Sia Kwang was found murdered too.'

'Sia Kwang? No, I hadn't heard. Just came in, as a matter of fact. Now, I remember that name! Someone told me that a peddler of curios called Sia Kwang associated with all kind of riff-raff, and warned me against having dealings with him. So one of his disreputable friends knifed him, eh?'

'His murder must be connected with the two other crimes. I don't mind telling you that I find myself up against a blank wall. It would greatly help me if I knew a little more about the persons who had relations with the victims, so as to give me at least an idea of the background of those appalling crimes.' He took a sip from his tea, and continued with a smile: 'I have a high opinion, not only of your

98

knowledge of antiques, Mr Yang, but also of your knowledge of your fellow men. Hence I came to you.'

Yang made a bow.

'I feel most flattered, Your Honour! I must stress, however, that, apart from my customers, I don't see much of the townspeople, and hear little of the local gossip. Since my wife died six years ago, and my two sons established their own business down south, I have lived only for my business and for my antiquarian studies. I lead a monk's life more or less, you know! I look after my simple needs myself, don't want clumsy maids around the house who break my best vases! At night no one disturbs me, for my assistant comes in for the day only. This is the kind of life I had always been looking forward to, sir. But it implies that I have lost touch with what is going on in this town!'

'The persons I am interested in are your customers, Mr Yang. What about Dr Pien, for instance?'

Yang emptied his cup, folded his arms and replied:

'Dr Pien collects jade. It stands to reason; old jade is supposed to possess medicinal qualities, hence most physicians and pharmacists develop an interest in it. The doctor has a small but fairly representative collection. He uses the pieces for study, he isn't interested in their commercial value at all. In this respect he is quite the opposite of his colleague in the drug business, Mr Kwang Min. Mr Kwang often has very valuable pieces, but he buys those purely as an investment, to be re-sold at the first opportunity. Mr Kwang is a keen businessman, first and foremost! Mr Kou Yuan-liang buys from him occasionally. Not me, his prices are too high.'

'I have met Mr Kwang. I thought he lived in the capital,' Judge Dee remarked.

'He does indeed. But he travels a great deal, and he visits Poo-yang at least every two months or so. But that's confidential, sir!'

THE JUDGE HAS TEA IN A CURIO-SHOP

'Why?'

'Because,' Yang replied with a sly smile, 'Mr Kwang also supplies Dr Pien's competitors here with drugs. Besides, Mr Kwang asked me to keep his visits to Poo-yang secret because of another reason too. He explained to me that he bought very cheaply a piece of land adjoining the Mandrake Grove some years ago—through the intermediary of Dr Pien. Mr Kwang made Dr Pien believe that he bought it just as an investment. In fact, however, Kwang has been sending his men there to gather the plant, on the edge of the grove. If Dr Pien knew that, he would of course ask Kwang to pay him a commission. As I said before, Mr Kwang is a very shrewd businessman indeed!'

'Quite,' Judge Dee said. He reflected that Kwang, without actually telling lies, had yet succeeded in giving him an entirely wrong impression of his activities. And, since that blandly courteous gentleman collected curios for gain, he might well have employed Tong or Sia to locate bargains for him—and for other purposes too, perhaps. He asked:

'Do you happen to know where Mr Kwang usually stays when he is here in Poo-yang?'

'If he doesn't stay on his junk, he rents a room in the Hostel of the Eight Immortals, sir. A very small, cheap inn,' he added with a deprecating smile.

'I know the place. Mr Kwang is certainly a parsimonious man!'

'Money means everything to him, Your Honour. He doesn't care a fig for antiques, for him it's just a side-line to make money. Mr Kou Yuan-liang—now there's a real collector for you! Doesn't mind what he pays as long as he gets the best! Can afford it too, the lucky fellow!' He pensively rubbed his chin, then resumed, somewhat diffidently: 'As to me, I am a mixture of both, more or less. My business is buying and selling, of course, but I fall in love with a piece now and then, and keep it for myself. Wouldn't part with it at any price. And, as I grow older, this weakness gets worse. Formerly I enjoyed inspecting all those superb things in Mr Kou's collection, used to go there at least once a week! But the last four five years or so I go there only when Mr Kou invites me, and then I never go farther than his reception room, I refuse to see his collection. Jealousy, pure and simple!' He shook his head with a wan smile. Suddenly he asked: 'By the way, sir, have you discovered a clue to the murder of the drummer of Dr Pien's boat, that fellow Tong Mai?'

'Not yet. As I told you just now, it's a baffling case. To return to Mr Kou, I have always heard that he has indeed a choice collection. The man has the eye of the connoisseur. That is proved also by the women he chose for himself. Although his First Lady has been ill for a long time, she still is a very handsome woman—I happened to meet her, last night. And I must say that his Second Wife, the Amber Lady, was also an outstanding beauty.'

Yang shifted uneasily in his chair. After a while he said, as if he were speaking to himself:

'Kou's eyes never fail him. I remember Miss Amber when she was still a small ungainly slave-girl in old Tong's household. But Kou bought her, taught her what clothes to wear, how to make herself up, how to do her hair, what perfume to use, and himself selected her earrings, necklaces and other finery. After one year she had developed into a perfect beauty. But Heaven decided that he didn't deserve to possess those two exquisite women. Now Mrs Kou is incurably ill, and the Amber Lady is dead.'

He stared straight ahead, pensively plucking at his short beard. 'It is not without reason,' the Judge spoke, 'that the Ancients said that he who strives after possessing perfect beauty thereby excites the ire of the gods.'

Yang did not seem to have heard the remark. Suddenly he looked the judge full in the face and said sharply:

'No sir, Kou didn't deserve it! Since we are talking confidentially, I may as well tell you that there's a queer streak in his character. Let me give you an example. Once he was showing me one of his best pieces of foreign glass, a priceless Persian bowl. While turning it round in my hands admiringly, I pointed out to him a small discoloration near the bottom and remarked with a smile: "It's the small flaw that gives beauty its finishing touch!" Kou took the bowl out of my hands, looked at the flaw, then smashed it to pieces on the floor. A crime, sir!'

'Mr Kwang would never have done that!' Judge Dee said dryly. 'Nor Dr Pien, I'd say. By the way, I vaguely heard that the doctor, despite his solemn manner, is really quite a gay blade—in a very discreet way, of course.'

'No, I never heard that he frequents the licensed quarters, sir. No one would blame him if he did, though, for it is well known that his wife is a real harridan. Although she didn't bear him a son, she never allowed him to take a secondary wife or a concubine.' He shook his head, then looked up and added quickly: 'But the doctor is a man of a staunch, sincere personality, Your Honour. He bears up wonderfully with his domestic troubles.'

'I also heard rumours that Dr Pien is in financial trouble.'

The curio-dealer darted him a quick look.

'Financial trouble? I should hope not! He owes me quite a bit of money. No, I can't believe that, he is a sound businessman, and he has a good practice too, all the notables of Poo-yang consult him. He regularly looks after Mr Kou's First Lady, you know.'

The judge nodded. He emptied his teacup, then put the fragile egg-shell piece carefully back on the table. For a while he silently caressed his long black beard. At last he spoke:

'Now that I am here I may as well ask your opinion on quite another matter. You are of course familiar with the famous story about the Emperor's pearl that was stolen about a hundred years ago. Have you any theories about that old mystery?'

'The search was so thorough, sir, that I am convinced that it was the Empress herself who took the pearl and concealed it about her person. Just to have an opportunity for having a few rivals in the Emperor's love tortured to death! That aim achieved, she threw the pearl in a deep well or somewhere. Many a tragedy takes place behind the golden gates of the Imperial Harem, Your Honour! Besides, why should somebody steal a thing that he could never sell?'

'Suppose that the pearl was really stolen, though, Mr Yang. Would there have been absolutely no way of turning it into cash?'

'Not within our Empire, sir. But, if the thief had good relations among the Arab or Persian merchants residing in Canton, he could sell the pearl perhaps to one of them—at a fraction of the real value of course—to be re-sold in a distant barbarian country. That would be the one and only way to dispose of it without getting into serious trouble.'

'I see. Well, I must go now, I still have to make the necessary preparations for the noon session. By the way, have you ever visited that ruined temple in the Mandrake Grove?'

Yang's face fell.

'Unfortunately not, Your Honour! There's no passable road through the dense forest, and the local people would resent attempts to get inside. I have a good description of it, though.' He got up, walked over the book-rack and took down a volume. Handing it to the judge, he said: 'This book was published privately by one of Your Honour's predecessors.'

Judge Dee leafed it through, then gave it back.

'We have our own copy in the chancery,' he said. 'Quite an interesting book. It gives a good description of the marble statue of the goddess.'

'What wouldn't I give to see that statue once!' the curio-dealer said wistfully. 'It is said to date from the Han dynasty and to have been carved from one single block of marble, together with the pedestal. The square altar standing in front of it is also of marble, it was there that they killed the young men dedicated to the goddess. An important relic of the past, sir! Couldn't Your Honour propose to the Ministry of Rites to have the forest cleared and the temple restored? If the Ministry would explain that portents have signified that the goddess is angry about the neglect of her temple, the local population wouldn't oppose the plan, I think. That temple could be made into one of the historic sites of our district, sir!'

'That's an excellent suggestion. I'll certainly keep it in mind. I don't like to have in my district a closed-off area shrouded in mystery. Heaven knows what may go on there!' He got up and added: 'Well, I am much obliged to you, Mr Yang!'

While the curio-dealer was conducting the judge downstairs he said:

'I'll go to the tribunal too presently, sir. Practically all the people concerned with the victims are my customers, so I feel it's my duty to attend the session!'

XIII

Back in the tribunal, Judge Dee went straight to his own residence in the rear of the compound. He felt hot and tired. He took a quick bath, put on a clean summer robe of white cotton, and placed a cap of thin gauze on his head. Thus attired he walked over to his private office. Sergeant Hoong was waiting for him there.

The judge took a fan of long crane-feathers from the wall and sat down behind his desk, fanning himself vigorously. Even the brief walk from the residence through the tribunal compound had made him perspire profusely again. He asked the sergeant briskly: 'Well, what's the news?'

'I was lucky, sir, I met a talkative young maidservant of Kou's household, in a vegetable-shop near by. It took me little trouble to find out from her that Mr Kou did indeed go out for a ride, very early this morning.'

'Does he do that often?' Judge Dee asked quickly.

'Never, sir! The maid said the servants were agreed that Kou went out in order to take his mind off the Amber Lady's death. She added that, despite the difference in age, Kou and Amber were very fond of each other, and that Amber always helped Kou to look after his First Lady. It was a very harmonious, happy household, she said.'

Hoong waited for some comment, but Judge Dee remained silent. Suddenly the judge sat up and pointed at two small oblong pieces of bamboo that were lying among the papers on his desk. 'When did those markers arrive?' he asked.

'They were brought a few moments ago by the corporal in charge of the South Gate, Your Honour.'

The judge examined them eagerly. They were of about

the same size, and each had the number 207 scrawled across its surface. But, whereas the figures of the one were put down laboriously in the clumsy manner of an uneducated man, those on the other betrayed the sure hand of an experienced writer; the latter also had a thin, nearly invisible groove across it, dividing the marker into two equal squares. The judge moistened his forefinger and rubbed the number off. Putting the piece in his sleeve, he said with a satisfied smile :

'I'll keep this marker. The other can be returned to the south gate. Well, let me tell you now about my visit to Sheng Pa's girl-friend, Miss Violet Liang.'

'What is she, sir? ' Hoong asked eagerly. 'Is she really such a refined, delicate girl? '

'Delicate isn't the first word that comes to mind,' Judge Dee replied wryly. 'She is a woman wrestler from Mongolia, and quite a formidable one too ! ' He told the sergeant the gist of their conversation, and wound up: 'Thus we know now that a cruel maniac is on the loose in this city, and that he employed first Tong, then Sia to procure women for his base lusts. And of course it is the same fiend who is responsible for the three murders.'

'That indicates that we can rule out your first suspect, sir; Mr Kou Yuan-liang, I mean. I could imagine that jealousy made him kill his adulterous secondary wife and her paramour. But Kou is certainly not the kind of man who indulges in maltreating women just for pleasure ! '

'I am not so sure about that, Hoong. To the outside world and even to his own servants Kou appears to be a cultured art-lover, and an affectionate husband, but it is quite possible that there's a perverse side to him. Such people usually conceal their depraved proclivities very well. That's why cases involving these perverts are always particularly difficult to solve. The only ones who would know his true

107

character would be, of course, his two wives. Viewed from this new angle, the story about Mrs Kou going out to visit a friend and suddenly losing her memory does not sound very convincing. What if in reality she was fleeing from her husband, who was habitually maltreating her? And that it was despair over the cruel torments inflicted upon her that unhinged her mind? I remind you also of the scars found on the Amber Lady's dead body, which could point into the same direction. I must say that in that case there were extenuating circumstances for her adultery and her planning to elope with Tong Mai.'

The judge slowly fanned himself for a while, then resumed:

'After my visit to Miss Violet Liang, I visited Yang in his curio-shop. Since Miss Liang had told me that the criminal was a collector of curios, I wanted to gather some information about Yang's client's. He gave me an interesting character-sketch of Kou Yuan-liang.' He told Sergeant Hoong about the incident with the Persian bowl, then continued: 'Kou destroyed a valuable antique just because it proved to have a small flaw. It's easy to imagine Kou's reaction on discovering that another valuable possession of his, namely the Amber Lady, had the most serious flaw a wife can have: infidelity.' He frowned and thought for a while. 'Yet there's a snag here! Assuming that Kou is a pervert of the type mentioned, would he then have had Amber killed by a hired underling such as Sia? Thus denying himself the pleasure of killing her with his own hands?' He shook his head impatiently.

'There's one point that would seem indeed to point to Kou, Your Honour. I mean that Kou employed both Sia and Tong for hunting out curios for him.'

'I learned from Yang,' Judge Dee said curtly, 'that Dr Pien and Mr Kwang Min also collect curios.'

The booming sound of the large bronze gong in the gate-house reverberated through the tribunal. It was the sign that the noon session was about to begin.

The judge rose from his chair with a suppressed sigh. Sergeant Hoong helped him to don his official robe of heavy green brocade, then handed his master the winged judge's cap of black velvet. While he was adjusting the cap in front of the mirror Judge Dee said:

'I'll conclude the session as soon as possible, Sergeant! Thereafter I want you to go at once to Sheng Pa and see what he has found out about those racing bets. You can tell him, by the way, that I personally put in a good word for him with Miss Liang. Then you go to the Hostel of the Eight Immortals, and ask the owner about Mr Kwang. How often he stayed there, how long, and what visitors he received. Also, whether he had any relations with prostitutes or courtesans and, if so, whether any of those women ever had complaints about him. I want the fullest possible information on that bland businessman.'

The sergeant looked astonished, but there was no time for questions. He pulled the door curtain aside and Judge Dee passed through and entered the court hall. As he ascended the dais and seated himself behind the high bench, the hum of voices in the packed hall died out. Sergeant Hoong, who had stood himself in his customary place on Judge Dee's right hand, bent over to him and whispered:

'The citizens of Poo-yang are eager to hear more details about the murders, sir!'

Nodding Judge Dee surveyed the hall. The headman and six of his constables stood in their appointed place, below the dais and facing the bench. They carried whips, clubs, chains and the other awe-inspiring paraphernalia of their office. On either side of the bench stood a lower table, each with two scribes behind it. They were moistening their writing-brushes to make notes of the proceedings. In the front row of the spectators Judge Dee saw Mr Kou and Dr Pien, standing side by side. Mr Kwang Min and the curio-dealer Yang stood in the second row. He rapped his gavel and declared the session open.

After he had called the roll, he delivered a statement on the discovery of the murder of the Amber Lady and of Sia Kwang, without going into detail. He said that, since the two crimes had occurred in one and the same place, the court was convinced that there was a connection, and that a thorough investigation was in progress.

When the judge had finished, Kwang Min stepped forward. He made a bow and began:

'This person——'

'Kneel down!' the headman barked at him, raising his whip.

Kwang gave him an indignant look, but he obediently knelt on the stone floor in front of the bench and resumed:

'This person, the merchant Kwang Min, has the honour to report that he has decided to reside on his junk, temporarily moored at the landing-stage near the west city-gate.'

'It shall be so recorded,' Judge Dee said. After Kwang Min had risen he suddenly added: 'You were not too communicative when I questioned you this morning, Mr Kwang.'

Kwang looked steadily at the judge. He said soberly:

'I was specifically ordered to be brief, Your Honour.'

'One can be brief and still to the point, Mr Kwang. I know where to find you, you may go.'

When Kwang had resumed his place among the spectators, Judge Dee announced a new regulation that had just come in from the capital, regarding the issuing of identity cards. While explaining the new rule he noticed the sultry heat. He was getting drenched with perspiration under his thick robe. As he was about to raise his gavel and close the session

MR KWANG IS QUESTIONED IN THE TRIBUNAL

two neatly dressed men approached the bench and knelt down. They gave their names and stated that they were shopkeepers. They had become involved in a dispute over the ownership of a piece of land. A few spectators left the hall. The judge saw Mr Yang among them.

He listened patiently to the lengthy explanations of both parties. Finally he dismissed them with the promise that he would have their claims checked in the land registry. Then an old pawnbroker came forward and lodged a complaint about two hooligans who had tried to intimidate him.

The pawnbroker was followed again by other persons. The citizens had evidently been saving up their problems for after the first five festive days of the month. Time dragged on. The greater part of the spectators were now leaving the court hall, including Dr Pien, Mr Kou and Mr Kwang Min. The hour for the noon rice was drawing near. Judge Dee turned round to Sergeant Hoong and said in a low voice:

'Heaven knows when I'll be through! You'd better go now and do the errands I told you about. I'll see you later, in my private office.'

When the judge was closing the last case, there was a sudden commotion at the entrance of the hall. Judge Dee looked up annoyed, then quickly straightened himself in his chair. He saw a strange procession coming towards the bench.

In front walked three strongly-built fellows. Their clothes were torn, evidently they had been badly knocked about. One held his hands to the sides of his head, his shoulders were covered with blood. Another held his right hand up with his left, his pale face distorted with pain. The third stumbled rather than walked, and kept his hands pressed to his stomach. He seemed on the verge of collapsing, but was kept moving on by vicious stabs in his back from a folded parasol, wielded by Miss Violet Liang. Neatly dressed in her

112

brown jacket and trousers, she strode along, her broad, copper-coloured face expressionless. Behind her came a plump young girl, gaudily dressed in a blue robe with large red roses. The left side of her face was bruised, the eye closed.

Arrived in front of the bench, Miss Liang barked an order at the three men, who sank down on their knees. The head-man uttered a curse and stepped up to her, but she pushed him back unceremoniously, snapping: 'I know all about the correct court procedure. You keep out of this!' And, to the girl: 'Kneel down, dearie, it's the rule. You don't belong to the Palace personnel, like me.' Then she looked up at the judge and began in an even voice:

'This person respectfully reports her original name as Altan Tsetseg Khatun. By Imperial Decree the Chinese sur-name Liang was bestowed upon her, and the personal name Violet. A wrestler by profession. These three men are deserters from a military Canal junk, at present exercising the profession of footpad. Their names are, from left to right Feng, Wang and Liau. The woman kneeling on my left bears the surname Lee, called Peony, a licensed whore —by Your Honour's leave.' Turning to the senior scribe, she asked: 'Have you got all that down?' As the old man nodded in speechless astonishment, she again addressed the judge: 'This person begs Your Honour to be allowed to file an accusation against the men, Feng, Wang and Liau aforesaid.'

Judge Dee stared silently at the imperturbable woman. Then he said curtly:

'The request is granted.'

'When this person had sat down to her noon rice in the back-yard of her dwelling, attended upon by her maid Rose, she heard a woman cry for help in the alley running behind the said back-yard. She vaulted over the wall, and saw these three men in the act of dragging along forcibly the woman here on my left. When the woman again shouted for help the man Feng gave her a fistblow in her face that closed her left eye and thereupon drew a knife. I saw that the onlookers disappeared round the corner, and therefore stepped up to the men and politely inquired what it was all about. At first they refused to answer, but when I insisted they informed me that the day before yesterday Sia Kwang, a vagrant student, had given them a silver piece and told them to abduct the woman Lee from the establishment she belongs to, and to convey her to the third house in the second street behind the old Taoist temple, owned by a woman called Meng. The men had chosen noon as a convenient time for executing this commission, since at that hour there are few people about. As a further precaution they had wrapped a piece of cloth round the woman's head, but while passing behind my house she had just succeeded in pulling down the said cloth. Since the three men confessed to the crime of abducting a woman by force, and since it had come to my knowledge that this court is interested in the activities of the said Sia Kwang, this person repaired to this tribunal at once, inviting the three criminals to accompany me, and bringing also the woman Lee, as a material witness. I beg Your Honour's favourable consideration.'

She made a bow, then remained standing there, her feet spread and leaning on her parasol. As soon as she had mentioned the address the woman was to have been taken to, Judge Dee had motioned the headman to come up to the bench. He had told him in an undertone to go there immediately with six armed guards, arrest the inmates of the house, and put them in jail. Now he said to Miss Liang:

'This court commends you for your prompt action, Miss Liang. Conscious of your duties as a law-abiding citizen, you took immediate and effective measures. You will now make a fuller statement as to what happened, in order to complete the record.'

'I obey Your Honour's command. When this person as previously stated asked these three men what it was all about, the second in the row, called Wang, aimed a fistblow at my head. I caught his arm and dislocated his shoulder while flooring him with a hip-throw. I took care, however, that the crash should only stun him and not break his back, so as not to prevent him from delivering testimony later if so required. The man Feng then trying to knife me, I took the knife from him and used the same for pinning his left ear to the nearest doorpost. He wouldn't keep still and his ear tore, so I was obliged to pin his other ear to the door- post. As he then employed obscene language and wouldn't give satisfactory answers to my questions, I had to prod him a bit here and there but I desisted directly after he had agreed to deliver a complete confession. That's all.'

Judge Dee half rose from his chair and looked over the bench at the three groaning men on the floor. The one on the right lifted his head and tried to speak. But he could bring out only a croaking sound.

'What happened to this third person?' he asked.

'Him? I was standing on him while questioning Feng. For when I was attending to Feng this third man called Liau tried to place a foul kick in my belly. Bah, these people are rank amateurs! I stepped aside, made a feint, and when he lifted his head I crushed his throat with a backhanded blow of the side of my hand. Since he then wanted to run away, I laid him on his back on the ground by the side of Wang and stood myself on top of him with one foot in his groin and the other on his head. I carefully refrained from stamping my feet, however, so as not to cause fatal injuries.'

'I see,' Judge Dee said. He caressed his side-whiskers for a while, then leaned forward and told Feng:

'Speak up, when and where did you meet Sia Kwang?'

The man let go of his lacerated ears. The blood began to ooze down again. 'Met him in the wine-house in the market!' he wailed. 'Day before yesterday it was. Never saw the bastard before. He gives us a silver piece, says there's more to come, after the job. We——'

'Did Sia say who was his boss?' the judge interrupted. The man gave him a bewildered look.

'Boss? He hadn't got no boss. It was Sia who paid us, wasn't it? We wanted to get the wench that night, but her place is full of customers and she is working, so we can't make it. Last night same story. This morning we go to the wine-house to ask Sia for more money, because it's such a hard job. But Sia isn't there. So we say we'll have another try at the woman at noon. We got her all right, but in the street we run into this . . . this . . .'

'Lady!' hissed Miss Liang, bending over close to the man's head.

'Keep that monster away from me!' Feng shrieked in a panic. 'Know what she did to me, after she had stuck the knife through my ear? She . . . she . . .' He broke down completely and burst out in sobs.

Judge Dee rapped his gavel hard on the bench.

'Answer my questions!' he ordered. 'Do you confess to the crime you stand accused of?'

Holding his bleeding ears the man gasped:

'I confess!'

His neighbour Wang pleaded guilty in a trembling voice. The third could only nod once, then he pitched forward on his face. Judge Dee said to the senior constable who had taken the place of the headman:

'Convey these three criminals to jail and have the coroner attend to their injuries. They shall be heard again after they have sufficiently recovered.' While the constables were dragging the three men off, the judge addressed the girl: 'I shall now hear your statement, Miss Lee.'

The plump girl wiped her bruised face with her sleeve. She replied in a soft voice:

'We were just sitting down to our noon rice, me and the three other girls belonging to the house. Then those three men come inside and knock our doorman down. Our owner asks what they want. One man hits him with his fist in his face. He says they want to borrow me for the day, they'll bring me back later tonight. They grab me, wind a piece of cloth round my head and face and drag me outside, kicking me all the time. In the street I go along quietly with them for a while, then I get one of my hands free. I pull the cloth down and shout for help. Then Miss Liang comes———'

'Had there been previous attempts at abducting you?'

'Never, sir.'

'Who of your customers could have a hand in this affair?'

She gave the judge a perplexed look. After having thought for a while, she shook her head and answered:

'I really don't know! I have been working there only one year, sir. I am the daughter of boatman Lee from up-river. My father got into debt and had to sell either the boat or me. My customers were shopkeepers and their assistants, from the neighbourhood. All nice fellows, I know them well. Why should they want to have me kidnapped, seeing that they could get all they want in the regular manner?'

'Quite,' Judge Dee said. 'Did you, besides receiving customers in the brothel, also go out to attend parties in restaurants or wine-houses?'

'Oh no, sir! I can't sing or dance, so I was never hired out for parties. But my owner sent me there sometimes just to give a hand serving the food, or to help our Number One changing her dresses.'

117

'Mention the parties you attended in that capacity during the last two months or so.'

When she had started on a long list, Judge Dee realized that this did not lead anywhere. The parties had been large, Kou Yuan-liang, Dr Pien and other notables had been present at more than one, also Yang the curio-dealer. And she remembered that Kwang Min had attended as a guest a small dinner given by a local drug-dealer. He asked:

'Did any of the guests pay special attention to you?'

'Never, sir. I was only a maid, wasn't I? The gentlemen spoke only with the courtesans from high-class establishments. They did give me tips, though. Quite large ones too, sometimes.'

'Are the names Tong Mai and Sia Kwang familiar to you?'

She shook her head. Judge Dee ordered the senior scribe to read out his notes of the proceedings. Miss Liang and Miss Lee agreed that they were correct and impressed their thumb-marks on the documents.

The judge addressed a few kind words to the two women, then he rapped his gavel and closed the session.

Miss Liang handed her parasol to the girl.

'You hold that over my head when we are outside, dearie,' she said. 'I am very sensitive to the sun, and a person of my status shouldn't go about unattended, anyway.'

She strode off, the girl meekly following behind her.

XIV

In Judge Dee's private office the senior scribe assisted him in changing into a cool houserobe of thin grey cotton. The judge told him to have his noon rice served there in the office, and thereafter bring him a basin of cold towels. When the headman would come back, he was to report at once.

Having given these orders, Judge Dee began to pace the floor, his head bent. He considered the latest developments. Sia Kwang had evidently hired the three ruffians on the orders of his principal, the unknown maniac. Would the woman of the house of assignation behind the Taoist temple know that man? It seemed too good to be true! Yet it did happen sometimes that a difficult case was suddenly solved by such a lucky chance. There was a knock on the door. He quickly looked up, expecting the headman to come in. But it was only the clerk, bringing a tray with a bowl of rice, soup, and a platter of pickles.

Judge Dee took his meal seated at his desk. He hardly tasted what he ate, his mind was occupied entirely with the three murders. He felt that the investigation had now reached the turning-point, for the murderer's motive had been established at last. At first he had considered greed as the motive, the criminal's aim being to steal the pearl and the gold. Then he had discarded greed as the main theme; assuming that jealousy was the motive he had reached the decision that the story about the Emperor's pearl had been a hoax. Now he had to discard also jealousy, at least as the main incentive, because it had been established beyond doubt that the basic motivation had been a perverse urge to hurt women, any woman. The element of greed was still

119

there, of course, as proved by the theft of the gold and the cornering of the racing-bets, and he still had to include jealousy. But these factors had now been relegated to a secondary place, the dominant element was perverted lust. That was bad, for when persons possessed by that urge found their schemes thwarted, they were liable to resort to violent action, disregarding the consequences.

The number of suspects had now been reduced to three persons known to him, with a possible fourth, as yet unknown. He heaved a sigh. If greed, jealousy, vengeance or any other of the well-known common motives had driven the criminal, his course of action would have been obvious: a painstaking, systematic investigation of the background of each of his three suspects, including their antecedents, their family, financial status and so on. However, since he was dealing with a maniac, there was no time for such a protracted investigation. For the criminal might kill again, at any moment, and any person. He would have to take action, at once. But what action, and against whom?

After he had laid down his chopsticks he remained sitting there, so deep in thought that he did not notice the stifling heat any more.

The clerk came back, carrying a large brass basin with towels soaked in cold, scented water. As the judge was wiping his face, the headman entered. Seeing his dejected face, Judge Dee asked anxiously:

'What happened?'

'We found the house without difficulty, sir. It's the former gardener's lodge of a large old mansion, deserted many years ago. The main building is only a ruin, but the gardener's house, located in the back of the terrain, is in a good state of repair. The old woman Meng was the only occupant. A charwoman came in the mornings, for the rough work. The people living in that neighbourhood suspected that the house was used for immoral purposes, they often saw men and women going in and out there late at night. But, since the house is standing apart on that deserted property, they couldn't see or hear properly what went on. Therefore nobody has the slightest idea who murdered her.'

'Murdered? Why didn't you say so at once, you fool? How was it done?'

'The old woman was strangled, Your Honour,' the headman replied unhappily. 'She must have had a visitor, and shortly before our arrival too, for the tea in the two cups we found standing on the table was still warm. Mrs Meng was lying dead on the floor, by her overturned chair. A silk scarf was wound tight round her neck. I loosened it at once, but she was dead and gone. I had the body conveyed here. The coroner is conducting the autopsy now.'

Judge Dee bit his lips. This was the fourth murder! Then he mastered himself and said in a flat voice:

'All right, headman. You did very well. You may go.'

In the door the headman nearly collided with Sergeant Hoong. The guards at the gate of the tribunal had told the sergeant about the new murder, and he was anxious to hear what had happened. He quickly sat down and asked:

'What does this mean, sir?'

'It means that we are dealing with an uncommonly clever and resolute opponent, Hoong. I'll tell you what happened in the tribunal after you had left.' After he had given the sergeant a detailed account of the exploits of Miss Violet Liang, he said: 'The criminal must have seen Miss Liang leading the three ruffians and the prostitute to the tribunal. The three men he didn't know, of course, for he had left the negotiations concerning the kidnapping to his henchman Sia. But he did recognize Miss Lee, whom he had earmarked as a future victim when he met her at some party or other. He concluded that Miss Liang had surprised the kidnappers, and they would mention in their confession the address they were to take their victim to. He went there at once and killed the old procuress.' The judge angrily tugged at his beard. Then he heaved a sigh and asked: 'Well, what did your enquiries bring to light?'

'Not very much, sir. I had a long talk with Sheng Pa. The man did his best, but he discovered only that the person who had been behind the cornering of the bets was somehow or other connected with the antique trade.'

'Again the antique trade! Holy Heaven, every single person connected with this case seems to dabble in curios!'

'As to Kwang Min, Your Honour, the innkeeper described him as a quiet man who never gave any trouble and who paid his bills on the dot. He checked his register together with me, and we found that Kwang had stayed there eight times during the past year. He always turned up unexpectedly, and never stayed longer than two or three days. He used to go out directly after breakfast and to come in again only late at night. He never received any visitors.'

'When did he stay there last?'

'About three weeks ago. Kwang occasionally told the innkeeper to get a woman for him, always specifying that he wanted an ordinary prostitute and not an expensive courtesan; that she needn't be especially good-looking, as long as she was clean and healthy, and moderately priced.' The sergeant made a face and went on resignedly: 'I went to the brothel near by, where the innkeeper used to order the women for Kwang from. I spoke with the girls who at one time or another had slept with Kwang. They hadn't much to say. They described Kwang as no better and no worse than most customers. He never asked for anything special, and it wasn't necessary to make any efforts to please him, because he never gave large tips anyway. That was all.' He paused, then asked curiously: 'Why did you want all those particulars about Kwang, sir? I would have thought that . . .'

He was interrupted by a knock on the door. The coroner came in. After he had greeted the judge he handed him a sheet of paper, saying:

'As Your Honour will perceive from this autopsy report, the woman called Meng was about fifty years old. Except for the weal round her throat, I didn't find any marks of violence on the body. I presume that the murderer, when he had tea with her, left his chair on some pretext or other and, as he was passing behind her, suddenly wound the scarf round her neck. The scarf had been drawn tight with such savage force that the silk went deeply into the flesh, nearly cutting through her windpipe.'

'Thank you. Have the corpse placed in a temporary coffin, and inform the next of kin. Let them come to fetch it as soon as possible, it wouldn't do to keep it above ground too long in this terrible hot weather. Has Mr Kou Yuan-liang fetched the body of the Amber Lady already? Yes? Good. See to it that Sia Kwang's family is informed too. I heard that his parents are living in the capital.' He passed his hand over his face, then asked: 'How are the three prisoners doing?'

The coroner pursed his lips.

'The one with the lacerated ears has also a few broken ribs and internal injuries. I set the other's dislocated shoulder and gave him a sedative, for he suffers also from concussion of the brain. These two can be questioned in a few days, I think. As regards the fellow with the crushed throat, it will take weeks before he can speak again—if ever!'

When the coroner had taken his leave, Judge Dee said to Sergeant Hoong:

'It would seem that the unlucky trio has received already

123

the punishment! Miss Violet Liang is not a person to trifle with. Violet, forsooth! Heavens, this heat is getting worse and worse! Open the window, Hoong.'

The sergeant put his head outside, then quickly stepped back and closed the window again.

'Outside it's hotter still, sir! The sky is leaden with low-hanging clouds, and there's no breeze stirring. I fear we'll be in for a severe thunderstorm shortly.'

The judge took a wet towel from the basin, wiped his perspiring face, and draped the towel round his neck. Pushing the basin across the desk towards Sergeant Hoong he said:

'Help yourself. Well, while eating my noon rice I went over the three murders. The fourth, that of the procuress Meng, does not materially alter my conclusions. I shall try to sum up for you the situation now, Hoong.'

'Before doing so, sir, I would like very much to hear why you are so interested in Mr Kwang's activities.'

'I'll be coming to Kwang presently. He plays an important role in one of my theories. But let's tackle all this systematically. Now then, these murders point to a ruthless maniac as the main criminal. There are no direct clues to his identity, and he has taken good care to remove all persons who could have testified against him. The Amber Lady, Tong Mai, Sia Kwang, the procuress Meng—all dead! So no witnesses, no clues! Add to that the recurrent motif of the antique trade, the story of the Emperor's pearl, and the sinister background supplied by the White Goddess in her impenetrable sacred grove, and you have all the elements that make an intriguing, lovely case! Lovely to discuss and theorize about I mean—while having a leisurely cup of tea after a substantial dinner, together with a few congenial friends! But confound it, we have to solve this case, Hoong! And quickly too, for if there's more delay the man who is behind all this will doubtless manage to invalidate even the few indirect clues we have, and if necessary kill again! '

Judge Dee greedily emptied the cup the sergeant had given him. He changed the towel round his neck for a new one, then continued in a business-like manner:

' As to that unknown maniac, my list of suspects is headed by three persons. Each had the opportunity, and for each I could imagine a compelling motive.

' Kou Yuan-liang is still the main suspect. My case against him is substantially the same as I have outlined to you already. Let's now try to reconstruct what happened if he is indeed our man. Kou employs Tong Mai to get him curios, and at the same time to procure him the victims for his base lust. Tong takes those women after dark and by a circuitous route to the place of the old woman Meng, and Kou himself goes there too, wearing a mask or ensuring by other means that he is not recognized. He pays his victims generously; therefore the risk of their making trouble is small. The only weak spot in Kou's method is that he must employ an assistant. And that assistant, Tong Mai, is a clever and enterprising fellow. Tong wants more and more money, probably threatens to blackmail Kou. On top of that Kou discovers that Tong has a secret liaison with the Amber Lady and that Tong is the father of her unborn child. Kou decides to kill both Tong and Amber. But he is a patient man, he waits for a suitable opportunity. As a first step, he dismisses Tong, doubtless with an ample bonus, and employs Sia instead. Miss Violet Liang told me that Sia is not as clever and enterprising as Tong, and therefore less liable to make trouble.

' Kou knows that the time for taking vengeance has come when Amber tells him the rigmarole about the Emperor's pearl. Since Kou is a learned antiquarian, he realizes at once that it is a hoax, a scheme by which Tong and Amber hope to get funds for eloping together. This is his chance.

'Kou summons Sia Kwang. He tells him not to go ahead with the scheme for kidnapping the prostitute Lee. Maltreating her would only have been a routine amusement, now his mind is on bigger things. Sia promises he'll warn the three ruffians that the deal is off. We know now that luckily for us, Sia didn't get round to that, but that's neither here nor there. Kou gives Sia a map of the deserted house and the pavilion, and tells him that Tong and Amber will meet there after the races, Amber bringing with her gold stolen from him, and that they plan to elope together. Kou proposes that Sia go there in Tong's place, kill the adulterous Amber, and bring back the stolen gold. Kou promises Sia a generous reward. Kou can afford that, for his plan includes the ultimate removal of Sia.'

Judge Dee took up his fan. Leaning back in his chair, he went on, slowly fanning himself:

'What happens last night? Kou poisons Tong Mai when he and Dr Pien entertain the crews of the dragonboats at Marble Bridge. Thereby Kou achieves a threefold aim. One, he takes revenge on his wife's lover. Two, he eliminates a troublesome assistant. Three, he nets a tidy profit from cornering the racing-bets. Sia Kwang keeps the appointment in the deserted house, kills Amber, and brings the gold back to Kou. Then Kou tells Sia that the gold was not exactly stolen, but that it was to be the payment for the Emperor's pearl, hidden by Tong somewhere in the pavilion, and that Tong and Amber had planned to flee with the gold *and* the pearl. Kou adds that he purposely hadn't told Sia about the pearl before, because he hadn't wanted Sia to tarry in the pavilion for a search, after the murder of Amber. Kou points out that it had been a wise precaution, for Amber had for some mysterious reason been followed to the deserted house by officers of the tribunal, who nearly caught Sia. Kou adds

126

that they'll still get the pearl. The next morning they'll go out there together and search the pavilion.

'This morning, at dawn, as soon as the city gates are open, Kou and Sia go to the deserted house separately: Kou on a morning ride allegedly to take him out of himself a bit, Sia disguised as a carpenter going out on an early job outside the city. Kou lets Sia search the pavilion, because that will give him a chance of killing Sia when he is off-guard, and also because the fact that the pavilion has been searched will bear out the rigmarole Kou told me about the pearl. At a suitable moment Kou smashes Sia's skull with a brick, throws the body into the ditch, and rides back to the city.

'Later this morning Kou attends the session of the tribunal. After he has left, he sees in the street Miss Liang leading her procession here. He doesn't know her or the three ruffians, but he does recognize Miss Lee. He realizes that something has gone wrong, and that now we'll learn from the kidnappers about Kou's secret haunt, the house of old Mrs Meng behind the Taoist temple. And Mrs Meng knows him. So Kou hurries out there and strangles her. Now everything has been nicely attended to. He has avenged himself on his unfaithful wife and her paramour, he has got his ten gold bars back, and, in addition, the winnings of the boat race. Tong, Sia and Mrs Meng, the only persons who could ever testify against him, are dead. Finish.'

The judge paused. Sergeant Hoong silently poured out a fresh cup of tea for him. Judge Dee took a sip, wiped off his face again with a cold towel, and resumed:

'If Kou is innocent, then he is a much-wronged man. In that case his First Lady really lost her memory because of a sudden attack of malignant brain-fever, and Amber's scars must date from the time when she was still a slave-girl; in some households those unfortunates are often harshly

127

treated. In that case Kou believed the story about the Emperor's pearl. It was plausible enough, I myself thought that it was true, at first. Well, let's now forget, for the time being, everything I said about Mr Kou, and concentrate on our second suspect, namely Dr Pien Kia.

'In the first place: what could have been the doctor's motive? I think it was a feeling of frustration that brought him to his depraved debauches, as an indirect protest against his domineering wife who did not allow him to take another woman in the house. The man had no other outlet, for his wife's jealousy and the decorum inherent in his profession precluded open association with prostitutes or courtesans. And perhaps there was a cruel streak in him anyway. We know really very little about all those things, Hoong.

'However this may be, at first Pien vented his perverted passion on common, uneducated women provided for him first by his henchman Tong Mai, later by Sia Kwang; he must have shifted from Tong to Sia for the same reasons as quoted in my theory about Kou. Now the terrible thing about such perverts is that they crave for ever stronger excitement. Coarse, vulgar women soon can't satisfy Pien any more, he wants to humiliate by his sordid passion refined ladies, and Kou's secondary wife, beautiful and cultured Amber, becomes the target for his vile lusts. He sees her regularly, for he is Kou's First Lady's physician, as the curio-dealer Yang told me. However, to maltreat the wife of a prominent citizen is no small matter, Pien has to bide his time. He tells Sia to watch affairs in the Kou household; if Sia can get the Amber Lady for him, only for one night, he will be richly rewarded.'

Judge Dee sat up and took a few sips from his tea. Settling back into his chair again he continued:

'In this second theory we must assign quite different roles to Tong and Sia. In the first theory we assumed that Sia

128

didn't know about the plan of Tong and Amber until Kou told him about it. Now, on the contrary, we must take it that Sia had learned from Tong about the latter having agreed to meet Amber in the deserted house, there to exchange a pearl for a large amount of gold. But Tong is a careful scoundrel, he did *not* tell Sia that the pearl was a hoax, and that he was planning to elope with Amber. Sia sees a chance for getting the reward Dr Pien promised him. He prepares a sketch-map of the deserted house and the pavilion on the basis of information wormed out of Tong, then he goes to Dr Pien and tells him that now the doctor can get the Amber Lady into his hands. If Dr Pien can manage to get Tong out of the way that night, he, Sia, is willing to go to the deserted house in Tong's place, and lock Amber up in the pavilion. Thereafter Pien can go there and have his way with the "chicken in the coop". Sia will take the gold and the pearl, and he and Pien will divide the loot. They'll arrange that the next morning the Amber Lady is discovered in the pavilion. Everybody, including Kou, will then ascribe her terrible experience to an outrage committed by vagrant rowdies.

'Dr Pien readily agrees with this proposal. He'll not only get the Amber Lady into his hands, but also ten gold bars—which nicely solves his financial problems. I doubt whether Pien believed the story about the pearl. He is clever enough to have put two and two together, and to realize that Tong had invented the story of the pearl because he was planning to elope with the Amber Lady. But that does not concern him.

'Pien puts poison in Tong's wine-cup during the entertainment at Marble Bridge. That rids him of a troublesome henchman and nets him a sizeable sum by betting against his own **boat**. Later the Amber Lady finds Sia waiting for her in the pavilion. He tries to overpower her, but she puts up resistance and suddenly draws a knife. In the ensuing scuffle Sia is wounded, and he kills her, either accidentally or on purpose. Anyway this killing will give him more power over Pien. Sia takes the gold, but my arrival prevents him from making a search for the pearl. Sia goes back to the city and reports his failure to Dr Pien. He tells the doctor that he wants more than the share agreed upon, for Pien is responsible for the death of Amber. Sia does not realize, however, that he is dealing with a ruthless maniac. Pien feigns to agree, and works on Sia's greed by remarking that it would be a pity to let the pearl go. Sia, who doesn't realize that the pearl can never be sold, lets himself be persuaded by Pien to go together with him to the deserted house this morning, in order to get the pearl. Pien lets Sia search the pavilion, then kills him. Give me another cup, Hoong, my throat is parched!'

While pouring out the tea, the sergeant asked:

'What would Dr Pien have done this morning, sir, after he had murdered Sia?'

'He would have concealed himself among the trees along the path leading to the villa, I think, waiting till Mr Kwang had passed by on his way to their appointment. The doctor would have given Kwang sufficient time for discovering the ransacked pavilion, then he would have gone there too. Before leaving his hiding-place, however the doctor saw you and me walk along there. That was even better, now he would have two witnesses! He followed us to the pavilion.

'Well, the rest is very much the same as I explained in my first theory. Dr Pien had the same opportunity as Kou Yuan-liang for recognizing Miss Lee in the street, for Pien also had left the session earlier. The doctor rushed to the north quarter and strangled Mrs Meng. To sum up: Dr Pien had to forgo his amusement with the Amber Lady, but he has got rid of two expensive and troublesome henchmen,

130

and all his financial troubles are over, for he has obtained ten gold bars and, in addition, a considerable sum won at the races. Neat case, no loose ends left.'

Judge Dee paused. He listened for a while to the distant rumble of thunder that came from outside. As he was replacing the wet towel round his neck again, Sergeant Hoong observed:

'This second theory, sir, seems to me more probable than the first, if I may say so. It is simpler, for one thing. And other points against Dr Pien are that he tried to maintain that Tong Mai had died from a natural cause, and that he told Your Honour a deliberate lie when he said that he had seen Sia go back to the city after the races.'

'Significant, but not conclusive,' the judge said. 'Tong Mai's symptoms seemed indeed to point to heart failure. And, since Sia's face is disfigured by a scar, Dr Pien may well have mistaken in good faith another man with a similar scar for Sia. If Pien is innocent, that is!'

'Who would have repaired the pavilion, Your Honour?'

'I am inclined to believe it was Tong Mai. He had lived there, and consequently knew the place thoroughly. He did not repair the pavilion in order to store the curios he traded in, however, as I wrongly assumed at first. The barred window, the heavy door, the new lock—all these precautions were not meant to prevent outsiders from entering the pavilion, but to prevent someone confined there from getting out! The pavilion was even better suited for secret debauches with unwilling victims than the house of the old procuress behind the Taoist temple. "No one will hear the chicken cackle," as Sia told Miss Violet Liang.'

Sergeant Hoong nodded. He thought for a while, slowly tugging at his thin goatee. Suddenly he frowned and said:

'Your Honour said that three suspects headed the list.

131

Would Mr Kwang Min be the third? I must confess that——'

He broke off. Hurried steps of nailed boots resounded in the corridor outside. The door opened and the headman came bursting inside.

'Dr Pien has been assaulted and nearly killed, sir!' he panted. 'Down the street here, in front of the Temple of Confucius!'

XV

Judge Dee gave the sergeant a startled look. He righted himself in his chair and asked the headman: 'Who did it?'

'The man escaped, Your Honour! Dr Pien is still lying in the street where he was knocked down.'

'How did it happen?'

'The doctor was attacked while walking along the street, sir, towards the bridge over the waterway. The ruffian knocked him down, but, just when he was going to take the doctor's money, Mr Yang, who had heard him cry for help, came rushing out of his curio-shop. The man let go of the doctor, and ran for it, with Mr Yang on his heels. But he had disappeared in the maze of crooked alleys on the other side of the waterway before Mr Yang could catch him. Mr Yang made sure that Dr Pien was still alive and conscious, then he called the gatekeeper of the temple and came here to warn us.' The headman took a deep breath, and resumed: 'Dr Pien insisted that he should not be moved until another doctor could verify that there were no dangerous fractures.'

Judge Dee rose.

'We'll go out there at once. Call the coroner, headman, and let your men bring a stretcher. Come along, Hoong!'

The sky was still covered by low-hanging, dark clouds. They walked quickly down the steaming hot street, keeping close to the high outer wall of the tribunal. Arrived at the Temple of Confucius, they saw a cluster of people gathered near the gatehouse. The headman roughly pushed the on-lookers aside to let Judge Dee pass.

Dr Pien lay spread-eagled on the ground, at the foot of the wall. Yang was placing a folded jacket under his head.

Pien's cap had fallen off, his topknot had become loose, and his long greying hair was sticking in moist strands to his livid face. There was a large lump above his left ear, the left side of his face was badly bruised. His robe, a mass of dust, was torn from shoulder to waist. As the coroner squatted down by his side the doctor muttered:

'Check chest, hips, right arm and right leg. My head is all right. The bruise is painful, but I don't think the temple has been damaged.'

While the coroner began to go over Pien's chest with his sensitive fingers, Judge Dee stooped and asked:

'How did it happen, doctor?'

'I was walking along here, on my way to see a woman in labour. In Halfmoon Street, over on the other side of the bridge. There was no one about. I . . .' He broke off, his lips twitched in pain as the coroner felt the ribs.

'The villain attacked him from behind!' the curio-dealer blurted out angrily.

'I suddenly heard furtive footsteps behind me,' Dr Pien went on in a weak voice. 'Just when I wanted to look round, I received a blow against the left side of my head that smashed me against the wall. I fell down, half-dazed. I vaguely saw a tall ruffian looming over me. I began to shout for help, but he silenced me by kicking me viciously. Then he bent over me and tore my robe loose. Suddenly he stopped. I saw him run away towards the bridge, with Mr Yang behind him.'

'He was a tall fellow, clad in a dark-brown jacket and trousers, sir!' Yang said excitedly. 'He had bound his hair up with a rag.'

'Could you see his face, Mr Yang?' Judge Dee asked.

'Got only a glimpse, sir. Rather round face, with short beard and whiskers. That's about it, isn't it, doctor?'

Dr Pien nodded.

'Do you as a rule carry much money on your person?'

134

the judge asked him. As Pien shook his head, Judge Dee asked again: 'No important papers?'

'A few prescriptions, and one or two receipted bills,' Dr Pien muttered.

The coroner rose. He said cheerfully:

'No need to worry, doctor! Your chest is badly bruised, but no ribs broken, as far as I can see. Right elbow is wrenched, and your knee too. I would like to examine you more carefully in my office.'

'Put the doctor on the stretcher,' Judge Dee told the coroner. And, to the headman: 'Send four of your men to Halfmoon Street. Let them make a thorough search for a ruffian as just described by Mr Yang. Fellow is left-handed.' Thereupon the judge turned to the gatekeeper and snapped at him: 'Didn't you see or hear anything? What were you doing? Did nobody ever tell you that you are supposed to guard the temple?'

'I . . . I had just dozed off, Excellency!' the frightened man stammered. 'In my lodge next to the gate, I was. I was roused by Mr Yang hammering on the door.'

'I would have been having my afternoon nap too,' Yang said. 'It so happened, however, that my assistant had been sorting out a rather valuable collection of jade pieces in the shop downstairs, so I went down to make sure he had locked everything away properly before he left for his noon rice. When I was down in the shop I heard a cry for help outside, and rushed out into the street at once. Saw the ruffian tearing at Dr Pien's robe. He heard me and ran. I went after him, but I wasn't fast enough. Old age is catching up with me, I am afraid,' he added with a rueful smile.

'You probably saved the doctor's life, Mr Yang,' the judge said. 'You may come with us to the tribunal now, and write out an official statement. Lower the stretcher, constable! And don't touch the doctor!'

135

He watched the efforts of the coroner and Mr Yang to get Dr Pien on to the stretcher. With Sergeant Hoong's help they got him comfortably established there. As the two constables were carefully lifting the stretcher up, the judge said in an undertone to Hoong:

'The time was well chosen. During the siesta few persons are about. And the quarter across the bridge is a veritable rabbit-warren, an excellent place to hide.' He motioned the sergeant and the headman to follow him.

While the three men were walking back to the tribunal, with the stretcher bearers and the coroner and Yang behind them, Judge Dee said to the headman:

'Take a horse and ride to the landing-stage as fast as you can. Board Mr Kwang's junk, and summon him to come to the tribunal. If he isn't there, you wait for him. Hurry up!' As the headman ran ahead, the judge whispered to Sergeant Hoong: 'You go to Mr Kou's house at once, and check whether he is taking his siesta!'

When Judge Dee was back in his private office, he sat down at his desk and poured himself a cup of tea. He emptied it in one draught, then leaned his elbows on the desk. Knitting his eyebrows he tried to bring some order in the ideas his mind was teeming with. Something was wrong about this latest development, something connected with a vague intuition he had felt all along about this case. His soaking wet, grey robe was clinging to his back and shoulders, but he did not even notice it.

After a long while he suddenly straightened himself. He muttered: 'Yes, that could be the solution! Everything fits —except the motive!' He sat back in his chair, and tried to make up his mind what would be the wisest course to follow. The explanation that had occurred to him was not beyond the bounds of probability; but was he justified to take action on the basis of an intuitive feeling only?

Surely a theory arrived at by careful, logical deduction should take precedence over mere intuition? Or could he work out perhaps a scheme that would enable him to test his intuition and his logical reasoning—both at the same time? Stroking his long beard he again sank into deep thought.

Thus the coroner found him when he came to report, half an hour later.

'Dr Pien is doing all right, Your Honour,' he said with satisfaction. 'I have put an ointment on his chest, bandaged it, and placed his right arm in a sling. He can walk—with a stick, that is. The doctor asked whether he could go home now, sir. He wants to take a good rest.'

'Tell him that he can take that rest here, in the tribunal,' the judge said curtly. Seeing the coroner's astonished look, he added: 'I want to ask him a few more questions, later.'

Not long after the coroner had taken his leave, Sergeant Hoong came in. Judge Dee motioned him to sit down on the stool in front of his desk, and asked eagerly: 'Did you find Mr Kou at home?'

'No sir. His house steward informed me that Mr Kou had said that it was too hot for taking a siesta inside, and that he would go to the Temple of the City god, to burn incense. The Amber Lady's coffin has been temporarily placed there, pending an auspicious date for the funeral. Mr Kou came back just now. I told him to stay at home, because Your Honour would probably want to summon him to the tribunal later.' Giving the judge an anxious look, he asked: 'What does the attack on Dr Pien mean, Your Honour?'

'It may well mean just what it appears to be,' Judge Dee replied slowly, 'namely an attempt at robbing the doctor. If that is so, then the incident doesn't invalidate my theory about Dr Pien's eventual guilt. If, on the other hand, it was meant as a murderous attack, then Dr Pien must be innocent; without realizing it himself, he must know something that could lead us to the real criminal—who therefore wanted to silence him. In that case we must concentrate on my theory about Mr Kou. His sentimental trip to the temple just now may have been a pretext to give him an opportunity for hiring a ruffian to kill Dr Pien. The doctor wanted to go home, by the way, but I ordered him to stay here, so as to prevent an eventual second attempt on his life. I am glad you instructed Mr Kou to stay home until further notice. That leaves only my third suspect unaccounted for, namely Mr Kwang Min.'

'So it was indeed Kwang who is the third!' Sergeant Hoong exclaimed. 'But why did you add him to the list of suspects, sir? It's of course true that Kwang could answer the description of Dr Pien's assailant, but you had selected him already before this new development had taken place.'

Judge Dee smiled faintly.

'I had to include Mr Kwang, Hoong! As soon as I had discovered the meaning of a missing domino.'

'A domino?'

'Yes. A double-blank, as a matter of fact. Last night someone purloined a domino from the set I and my ladies were playing with on board my boat. The only persons who had an opportunity for taking that domino were Kou, Pien and Kwang. Pien and Kou when they came on board to report to me that the dragonboats were ready to start; the maid who was serving tea had then pushed the dominos in the pool aside, turning some of them with their face up. And Kwang had the opportunity when he came up on deck while I and my ladies had interrupted our game and were standing at the railing, admiring the festive water scene.'

'But why should the criminal want a domino, sir?'

'Because he has an alert mind,' the judge answered with a wan smile, 'much more alert than mine, as a matter of

138

fact! When he saw a double-blank domino lying on the table, he was struck by its close resemblance to the markers used by the guards of the city gates. He saw that at once, but it took me quite some time before I realized it! It flashed through his mind that it would be awkward if his hench-man Sia Kwang, returning to the city after closing time, should have to prove his identity to the guards at the south gate. If any inquiries were made later regarding persons returning to the city at a late hour, either in connection with Tong's murder or the maltreatment of the Amber Lady in the deserted house, the guards might remember Sia, especially because of that scar on his face. The criminal there-fore purloined the domino, on the spur of the moment. Later, he scrawled an arbitrary number on it, and gave it to Sia. Sia actually used it when he came back to the city to report to his principal what had happened in the pavilion. For the corporal at the south gate returned the false marker to me.'

'The criminal made a bad mistake there,' the sergeant observed.

'Not too bad. He couldn't have known that I take dominoes so seriously that one missing piece would be enough to set me thinking about the implications. Well, enough of theorizing! We must set to work now, for there is much to do, and little time. We really ought to initiate an extensive investigation into the background and move-ments of all the suspects, of course, but unfortunately there's no time for that. We can't afford to have a fifth murder! We have to take action, but I can't do anything before we have located Kwang. Go and have a look whether our head-man has turned up yet!'

The sergeant left hurriedly to make inquiries with the guards in the gatehouse. Judge Dee got up from his chair and walked over to the window. He pushed it open and leaned outside. He noticed with satisfaction that there seemed to be a faint current of air about. Then he bestowed a pensive glance upon the rock-garden. The small tortoise was happily plodding along among the plants that bordered the miniature goldfish pond. He moved his sturdy small legs with a purpose, his head eagerly stretched out. The judge turned round when he heard Sergeant Hoong come in.

'Our headman hasn't come back yet from the landing-stage, Your Honour.'

'I hope Kwang hasn't run away!' Judge Dee said worriedly. Then he shook his head and added: 'No, he won't have fled. He is much too clever for that.' He took his fan of crane-feathers, sat down again and resumed: 'While waiting for Kwang I may as well explain my theoretical case against him. Then you'll know exactly where we stand as regards the three gentlemen who head our list.'

The judge draped a new wet towel round his neck.

'I assume,' he began, 'that in the capital Mr Kwang Min leads an exemplary life. It is on his frequent business trips that he gratifies his depraved lusts. He is an uncommonly clever man, he keeps his perverted pleasures secret, very secret. He even takes the trouble to build up in the hostels he stays in the reputation of a perfectly normal person, a man who now and then has his fling with a professional woman, ordered from the innkeeper in the regular manner —healthy and cheap. But through his interest in the antique trade Kwang has come to know during his visits to Pooyang the students Tong and Sia. He employs first Tong, then Sia for his real pleasures—not so healthy and not so cheap. The same interest in antiques brings Kwang into contact with Kou Yuan-liang; Yang, the curio-dealer, told me that Kou occasionally bought from Kwang. We know that the Amber Lady acted as her husband's secretary, sorting out and cataloguing his antiques, so Kwang must have met her a few times while visiting Kou. Kwang wants

Amber, and for the same reason as I mentioned in my theory regarding Dr Pien: the urge to maltreat and humiliate a refined lady. Kwang orders Sia to warn him as soon as the youngster sees a possibility for delivering the Amber Lady into Kwang's hands.

'Some days ago Kwang must have informed Sia by letter that he would be arriving at Marble Bridge yesterday morning. Anticipating Kwang's wishes, Sia had hired the three ruffians to abduct the prostitute Lee whom Kwang had singled out as a future victim; Kwang had seen her at a party here, during one of his previous visits to Poo-yang. Yesterday morning Sia hurried to Marble Bridge. He told Kwang about his arrangements for the kidnapping of Miss Lee, but also the big news: Kwang can get the Amber Lady, the selfsame night. Sia then tells Kwang about the planned rendezvous of Amber and Tong in the deserted house for selling the pearl, and adds that he is willing to go there instead of Tong. Kwang agrees with enthusiasm, for as well as amusing himself with the Amber Lady, he will get ten bars of gold. Kwang probably does not believe the story about the pearl, but those doubts he keeps to himself. His first concern is how to get rid of Tong Mai. Sia informs him that before the races the crews will be entertained at Marble Bridge, and that Tong will be there as Dr Pien's drummer. That solves Kwang's problem. He sends a note to Dr Pien asking him to come and see him on his junk. Pien answers that he is busy, but that he'll come later in the afternoon. All the better. Kwang lets Pien take him to the entertainment, and there he puts the poison in Tong's wine-cup. Sia will keep the appointment in the deserted house, Kwang will proceed there as soon as Sia has reported to him that the Amber Lady has been locked up in the pavilion. Kwang will "discover" the distressed woman there the next morning, when he meets Dr Pien in the deserted house to have a look at his property. Since Kwang is a greedy man, he gives Sia the necessary instructions regarding the cornering of the bets. Finally, he orders Sia to cancel the agreement with the three ruffians. For Kwang's mind is now on higher things than maltreating a common prostitute.'

Judge Dee fell silent. He listened for a while to the roll of thunder. It seemed to be quite near, this time.

'Why did Kwang visit your barge last night, sir?' the sergeant asked.

'I have been asking myself that same question, Hoong! The explanation must be that Kwang wanted to establish the fact that he was there during the boat race, and didn't return to Marble Bridge till late in the night. The boatmen were drunk and Sun ill, so it would be difficult to trace Kwang's movements. However that may be, Kwang purloins the domino, hands it to Sia, then hurries back to Marble Bridge. Later in the night he meets Sia there, and Sia informs him that all has gone wrong: that he had to kill the Amber Lady, and got only the gold because my arrival prevented him from making a search for the pearl. Kwang regrets the lost hours with Amber, but—and this is perhaps even more important to him—he has gained ten gold bars. Then we get the same story as before: Kwang persuades Sia to go to the deserted house this morning, disguised as a carpenter, in order to make a thorough search for the pearl. Kwang has a good reason for his own presence there, namely his appointment with Dr Pien. After Sia has searched the pavilion, Kwang kills him. The last phase, the murder of the old procuress, is the same as I outlined in my theories regarding Kou and Pien. That's all.'

Judge Dee wiped off his face with a new towel, and Sergeant Hoong followed his example. It was stifling hot in the small office. After a while Hoong remarked:

'A small point in Kwang's favour is his becoming so

violently sick at seeing Sia's dead body. That's not so easy to feign.'

The judge shrugged.

'Kwang politely turned his back on us, and our attention was concentrated on our gruesome discovery. Kwang may have rammed his finger into his throat, for all we know!'

There was a knock on the door, and the headman came in. He began with a contented smile:

'I had to wait a long time, sir, but I got Mr Kwang! The captain of the junk told me that Mr Kwang and Mr Sun had gone into town directly after the noon rice, to do some shopping. Mr Sun came back alone, he said that Mr Kwang had some business on the waterfront. I went there at once, traced him to a small pharmacy, and collared him there. He is waiting now in the guard room.'

'Good! Where is Dr Pien?'

'The doctor is having a cup of tea with the coroner, sir, in the chancery. He has dictated his report on the assault. I have here also Mr Yang's written statement. Mr Yang has gone back to his shop.'

The judge glanced through the two papers. He handed them to the sergeant and asked the headman:

'Did your men catch that footpad?'

The headman's face fell.

'No, Your Honour. They questioned lots of people in Half-moon Street, and searched all likely places. But they found no trace of the ruffian.'

He gave the judge an anxious look expecting a sharp rebuke. But Judge Dee did not scold him, he silently tugged at his side-whiskers. Then he spoke:

'Tell Mr Kwang that I shan't see him now, because I want Mr Kou and Dr Pien to be present when we have our talk. I want to keep that discussion quite informal, therefore I have decided to hold it in Mr Kou's house. That is much

143

better than here in the tribunal. You can now take Mr Kwang and Dr Pien to Mr Kou's residence, in a closed palankeen. Tell Mr Kou that I want to hold our meeting in his library. That is a quiet room in a secluded section of his mansion, the same where Mr Kou received me last night. You may inform Mr Kou that I myself shall proceed there as soon as I have dealt with a few routine matters here. Have you got all that?' As the headman bowed obsequiously, the judge went on: 'After you have delivered Mr Kwang and Dr Pien to Mr Kou's house, you come back here at once for further instructions.'

When the headman had left, Sergeant Hoong asked eagerly:

'Does Your Honour expect that if those three are cross-examined together, the guilty one will betray himself?'

'That's what I am hoping, at least! I have an errand for you now, Hoong. I need a wooden hand.'

'A wooden hand, sir?'

'Yes. Go to Mr Yang's curio-shop and ask him whether he can help us. He'll certainly have some spare hands of Buddhist statues lying about. As a rule those are carved from a separate piece of wood, and added to the statue only after the body has been completed. I want a left hand, life-size or larger. I want him to paint that hand white, Hoong, and to put on the forefinger a brass ring with some cheap red stone. You will explain to Mr Yang that I need that hand as an exhibit, during a meeting with Dr Pien and Mr Kwang which I am going to hold in Mr Kou's library tonight.'

A flash of lightning lit up the paper window, followed almost at once by a deafening thunderclap. Judge Dee resumed quickly:

'You had better take a sedan-chair, Hoong, in case the rain should start. When you are back I shall explain what I am planning to do. Get going now, time presses!'

XVI

Dusk had fallen when the perspiring chair coolies put Judge Dee's large official palankeen down in the front courtyard. Six enormous lanterns of oiled paper hung from the eaves of the surrounding buildings, each bearing in large red letters the legend: 'Kou's Residence'. Their light shone on Kou Yuan-liang's anxious face as he came running towards the palankeen, accompanied by his house steward. The two men had been standing in the courtyard for a long time, waiting for the magistrate's arrival.

Judge Dee descended from the palankeen, followed by Sergeant Hoong. Mr Kou made his deepest obeisance. The judge nodded, then addressed him affably:

'I am sorry that urgent official business detained me in the tribunal, Mr Kou! Mr Kwang and Dr Pien have arrived already, I suppose?'

'Indeed, Your Honour. We were getting worried, sir; we feared that the storm might start while Your Honour was still on the way here.' As there was a flash of lightning, followed by a low rumble, he added quickly: 'This way, please!' and hurriedly conducted them inside.

He took Judge Dee and the sergeant through the winding corridor to his library in the back of the compound.

When the judge stepped inside he saw with satisfaction that the library was exactly as he remembered it from the previous evening. The large, sparsely furnished room was lit by six tall candelabras, arranged in three pairs between the four windows in the back wall. To the left of the door stood a large cabinet with a fine display of antique porcelain and foreign glass. The wall on the right was taken up entirely by high racks, loaded with books and manuscript rolls. A thick-piled blue carpet covered the floor. In the centre stood a heavy square table of polished ebony, and four chairs of the same material. Dr Pien and Mr Kwang were sitting at the round tea-table in the farthest corner, by the window on the right.

They rose hastily and came to meet the judge, Dr Pien supporting himself on a bamboo stick. Judge Dee was glad to see that the long wait in the hot, close room had evidently upset the two men. Their faces were haggard in the candle-light and their thin summer robes clung to their wet shoulders. He called out jovially:

'Resume your seats please, gentlemen! Glad to see you are doing well, doctor. You should be careful though, don't move about too much!' He took his seat at the tea-table, and continued: 'I am so sorry to have kept you waiting, but you know how it is, in the tribunal . . .' Cutting short the polite murmurs of Mr Kou, he told him: 'My assistant shall help your steward with the tea, Mr Kou. It's a bit hot here, I must say, but you were right in keeping the windows shuttered. We'll have a real tempest before long, I dare say. But, taking all in all, we shouldn't complain about the climate here, you know. When I think of the severe winters up north . . .'

There was a further exchange of polite remarks while the steward and Hoong served tea. The judge took a sip and said with a broad smile:

'This tea is truly excellent, Mr Kou! As one would expect in the house of a man of such elegant taste!'

Seeing Judge Dee's high good humour the others had visibly brightened up. Dr Pien wiped the moisture from his forehead and asked:

'Is there any news about the rascal who assaulted me, Your Honour?'

146

'Not yet, Dr Pien, but my men are at it. Don't worry, we'll get the scoundrel!'

'I deeply regret to cause this extra trouble,' the doctor said contritely. 'Your Honour must be very busy just now, with that astounding mur——' He broke off in the middle of the word, cast a quick glance at Kou, and corrected himself: '—with other, graver matters.'

'Yes, I am being kept very busy indeed. And that brings me to the purpose of the present conference. I have requested you to come here, gentlemen, because I am in need of your advice.' Turning to Kou, he went on: 'I trust that you'll forgive me for choosing your residence, during these sad days of mourning. But since you are so directly concerned in the awful tragedy, I hope that you will . . .' He did not finish his sentence. As Kou gravely inclined his head, the judge went on: 'You can tell your steward to leave, Mr Kou. I see that refreshments are standing ready on the side-table. My assistant will attend upon us.'

Judge Dee waited till the steward had left. Then he leaned forward in his chair and resumed:

'I have always taken the view that a magistrate should share his problems with the notables of his district, so as to be able to profit by their knowledge and experience, and to solicit their advice.' He bestowed a smile upon Kwang and added: 'It's true that you are not a resident, Mr Kwang, but since you visit our district so frequently, I took the liberty of including you too.' Ignoring Dr Pien's astonished look, he continued: 'I don't mind telling you frankly, gentlemen, that I am badly needing your advice now. Four murders have been committed in our city, and I am completely in the dark as to the identity of the person who is responsible for these foul crimes. A detailed investigation is indicated. The purpose of this conference is to draw up together the lines along which my inquiries might be most profitably conducted. I expect that it will take many days before we can hope for results, but that does not matter. Slow but sure, eh, as the saying goes.'

Kwang raised his thin eyebrows.

'Does that mean, sir,' he asked, 'that I shall have to stay here in Poo-yang all that time?'

'Not necessarily, Mr Kwang. Sometimes a most baffling case is solved unexpectedly by a lucky chance, you know! Let's have some of those cold fruits, Sergeant! And no talk about business while we are eating, gentlemen, please!'

While they were tasting the delicious slices of iced fruit served by Sergeant Hoong in bowls of antique coloured porcelain, Mr Kou thawed somewhat. When he had emptied his bowl, he related an interesting story about a faked painting. Then Judge Dee told of an amusing case he had dealt with on a former post. He told the story well, and all laughed heartily. Despite the oppressive heat there was a pleasant, relaxed atmosphere now. When the sergeant was about to refill the teacups, Judge Dee suddenly rose and said briskly:

'Now we had better get down to business, gentlemen!'

He walked over to the table in the centre of the library. He sat down in the armchair at the end where he had the windows on his left and the door on his right. He motioned the others to take the three chairs that Sergeant Hoong was placing along the opposite side of the table. Dr Pien took the one in the middle, straight across from the judge. Mr Kwang sat down on the doctor's right hand, Mr Kou on his left.

Judge Dee pushed the large silver candelabra aside so that it stood to the left of him. He said testily:

'Heavens, it's really hot! Put those candles along the wall there out, Hoong! They only make the heat worse! And their light bothers me. I am having trouble with my eyes nowadays, gentlemen. The glare of the sun, I suppose. Let me see whether I have brought my eyeshade along.' He

148

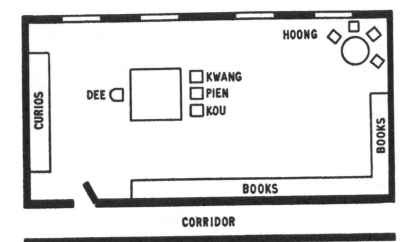

felt in his sleeve and took out an envelope. 'Good gracious!' he exclaimed, 'I haven't even opened this letter! It was delivered to the tribunal just when I was leaving. Marked "personal and urgent", eh? Will you excuse me a moment?'

He tore the flap open and extracted a folded sheet of paper. It was a long letter in a very small, crabbed hand-writing. Glancing through the beginning, the judge muttered: 'Fellow says that a niece of his, serving as maid somewhere, was abducted and came back sorely maltreated. Well, well, the poor girl must have fallen into the hands of a maniac.'

He read on silently for a while.

'The man says,' he resumed, 'that she got a glimpse of her tormentor. Quite a well-known person here, it seems. Therefore, he says, he hesitated long before reporting to me, postponed it time after time. Since he feels, however, that such things shouldn't be allowed to happen in a well-administered city, he asks for an immediate investigation, suitable measures to prevent . . . yes, yes, we know all that. He should have reported at once, of course. Where does he mention the offender's name now?' He brought the letter closer to his eyes, then shook his head and said: 'Can't find it, never saw such bad handwriting!' Looking up, he added: 'Here, you had better read the rest aloud for me, Mr Kou!'

He made to hand the letter to Kou, then suddenly checked himself. He said with an apologetic smile:

'No, I shouldn't show official letters to outsiders, I suppose! I shall study it afterwards.'

He folded the document up and put it back in his sleeve.

'People should think twice before making such preposterous accusations!' Mr Kwang said, annoyed.

'I wouldn't say off-hand it's preposterous,' Judge Dee remarked, suddenly grave. 'As a matter of fact I have grounds for suspecting that the criminal we are looking for is the same type of maniac as this letter refers to.'

Leaning back in his chair, Judge Dee watched the three men across the table. Their faces, just within the cone of light thrown by the candle, had become tight. The agreeably relaxed mood had dropped away from them.

The judge quietly surveyed the room. Sergeant Hoong had retreated to the round table in the corner. He sat there, staring at the small candle on the tea-tray. The rest of the room was a mass of black shadows. The smell of the snuffed-out wall candles hung heavily in the close air.

Judge Dee let the uncomfortable silence drag on for a while. Casually turning his head, he looked at the door. It was very dark there, he could only distinguish the thin ray of light that came through the slit between door and threshold, from the lamp in the corridor. If someone had been standing outside to listen, he would have set the door ajar; the judge had given him plenty of time. The judge thought that his intuition must have been wrong, after all. That meant that he could now concentrate on the three men in front of him.

'I said just now,' he resumed, 'that I suspect the criminal to be a maniac. A dangerous maniac. I have come to that conclusion because . . .'

He broke off in mid-sentence. He thought he had heard the door being closed softly. He quickly looked round to the right. He saw nothing but the thin ray of light over the threshold. His ears must have deceived him. He cleared his throat and went on:

'I think I have a fairly clear idea of the criminal's personality. Mainly thanks to a curious mistake he made.'

He noticed that Kou was shifting uneasily in his chair. Dr Pien looked fixedly at the judge, his thin lips tightly compressed. The bruised, blue left side of his face contrasted sharply with the pallor of his skin. Kwang had recollected himself, he had now assumed an expression of polite interest.

'Everyone who murders in cold blood,' Judge Dee went on in an even voice, 'thereby proves himself to be abnormal. And if the motive is perverted lust, then such a man is in fact continually on the verge of becoming insane. Such a person lives a terrible life. He must keep up appearances and go on with the normal daily routine, all the time trying to keep under control the compelling urges that torment him. Convicted lust murderers have related all this in their confessions. They have described in detail their desperate struggle to retain their mental balance. They said they were visited by horrible hallucinations, that the forces of darkness were constantly lying in wait for them, that the ghosts of their victims persecuted them. I remember one case I dealt with where . . .'

He paused and listened intently. Now he was sure he had heard the door close. Out of the corner of his eye he saw something move in the darkness, over in the corner, between the door and the cabinet with the curios. Someone had come inside. This was a possibility he had overlooked. He had counted on the intruder to set the door ajar so as to overhear what was being said. And that the man would betray himself only later—much later. But it couldn't be helped now. He had to go on.

'When I interrogated that murderer he maintained that every night the severed hand of the woman he had killed and mutilated came crawling over his breast, trying to strangle him. He——'

'Must have been only a dream!' Dr Pien blurted out.

'Who knows!' Judge Dee said. 'I may add that the man was found strangled in his cell, the morning before the execution. Of course I stated in my report to the higher authorities that he had done it himself half-crazed by fear and remorse. And perhaps he did just that. On the other hand . . .'

He shook his head doubtfully and considered for a few moments, stroking his long beard. Then he continued:

'Anyway, it explains why in our present case the murderer made that mistake. Was compelled to make it, I should say perhaps—since he risked stirring up forces that are better let well alone. The murder of Tong Mai may have pleased the White Goddess, it may have reminded her of the ancient human sacrifices, when the veins of a young man were cut on the altar before her, and his blood sprinkled over her marble statue. But the murder of the Amber Lady, a woman like herself, and hard by her sacred grove—that seems a reckless taunting of forces we know very little about, really.' He paused, shrugged his shoulders and went on: 'However this may be, I have proof that the murderer made a mistake that can be explained only by a very strange lapse of memory. He is an extremely clever man, but he had apparently completely forgotten that on the scene of the crime he——'

'Which crime?' Mr Kou asked hoarsely. He quickly looked at the two others, then stammered to the judge: 'Please excuse my . . . my interruption. But . . . I mean to say, there were four murders, were there not?'

'There were indeed,' Judge Dee said dryly.

A distant roll of thunder was heard outside.

'You mustn't let this awful weather get hold of you, Mr. Kou,' Kwang Min remarked. It was meant to be reassuring, but his voice sounded unnaturally high in the still room.

'I think I saw the door move, sir!' a worried voice suddenly spoke up. 'Shall I have a look?'

It was Sergeant Hoong. He had left his corner and was coming up behind the three men at the table.

For a moment the judge did not know what to do. For a special reason he had not told the sergeant that his plan included the possibility of a secret listener. Apparently Hoong had seen the intruder leaving, and had got the wrong impression that he was coming inside. But the judge could take no chances. If the man were still in the room, he must not know that the judge was aware of his presence, else all had been in vain. He said sharply to the sergeant:

'Must have been a trick of the light, Hoong! Go back to your place and don't interrupt me!' He thought he heard the sergeant's cotton robe rustle as he went back to his corner. No, it wasn't Hoong's clothes! The sound came from behind him, he now heard it quite distinctly. It was a slithering sound, as if of silk. Someone was coming up behind him. He quickly searched the faces of the three men opposite, but realized at the same time that they could not see beyond him. His own face was just inside the light circle, the rest must be only a mass of black shadows to them. He would have to be quick.

153

'Well,' he resumed, 'for the moment I won't dwell on that curious oversight of the murderer. I shall mention another fact that is even more important. The murderer employed as henchman the vagrant student Sia Kwang, and Sia talked too much when in his cups. I have traced a vaga-bond who used to drink with Sia. That man said that Sia's principal employed also another helper. But of a quite differ-ent type. He . . .'

Again Judge Dee heard the slithering sound, now quite near. His muscles grew tense. He had counted on the danger coming from the right, where he could half see an attacker and defend himself. But now someone was breathing directly behind him.

The three men had noticed the sudden change that had come over Judge Dee's face. Pien brought out in a strangled voice:

'What's the matter, sir? Why——'

A loud thunderclap made him give a violent start.

It flashed through Judge Dee's mind that he had better jump up now and grab the intruder who was standing behind him. But no, that person's mere presence was no proof of his guilt. He could say that he had not wanted to disturb the conference, and that he therefore . . . Some-thing was stirring in his sleeve. No, he had to go on as planned. Perspiration was streaming down his face but he did not notice it. He spoke in a voice he hardly recognized as his own:

'That third man was a well-known citizen. Yet he was not only concerned in the murder of Tong Mai, he was also directly responsible for the strangling of the old procuress. She was strangled from behind, her weak, white hand clutched in vain at the silk cutting her throat. She died a violent death, only a few hours ago. If her ghost walks among us now, it . . .'

154

Suddenly he uttered a suppressed cry. Sitting up in his chair, he stared with wide eyes over the heads of the three men opposite and shouted at the sergeant the pre-arranged question:

'Who is standing there behind you, Hoong?'

Dr Pien turned round in his chair abruptly, Kou and Kwang looked behind them with choked curses. Sergeant Hoong had jumped up, now he came running towards them, wildly waving his arms. Judge Dee quickly took a bulky object from his left sleeve. Placing it on the table's edge he exclaimed, horrified:

'Look! Help me, for Heaven's sake!'

As the three men turned to him again, Hoong stood himself close behind them, groping in his sleeve. At the same time Kou and Pien let out a scream of terror. Kwang moved his lips spasmodically, but no sound came forth. All three stared aghast at the white hand that seemed to be clutching at the table's edge. The red stone on the forefinger shone with a wicked gleam as the hand slowly crawled towards the candle. It was a severed hand, the wrist ended in a red, ragged stump. It changed its course, now it began making for the three men.

Judge Dee half rose. Dr Pien sprang up, his chair crashed to the floor. His distorted face was livid. His eyes glued to the moving hand, he shrieked: 'I didn't kill her!'

He turned round and stumbled into Hoong's arms. 'Help me!' he shouted. 'I didn't kill her. Only Tong. By mistake! I had been told that . . .' He broke out in convulsive sobs.

The judge had not heard him. Having half risen from his chair, he had turned his head while raising his right arm to ward off whatever danger was threatening him from behind. But he had suddenly frozen in that attitude. He was staring up in nameless terror at the other white hand that had appeared from the shadows behind him, close to his head.

XVII

For one terrible moment Judge Dee thought he had wantonly evoked the dead. Then the white hand rose. He saw with immense relief a black sleeve. The hand pointed at the door that now was standing ajar, letting in the light from the lamp in the corridor outside. It revealed a large man, who stood there leaning against the doorpost.

A soft but firm voice spoke up close by the judge:

'You can't hide from me. Come nearer!'

The voice startled Kou and Kwang from their horrified contemplation of the hand on the table. Dr Pien let go of Hoong and turned round. All three looked in speechless astonishment at the tall woman, clad in a long-sleeved black robe, who had appeared in the light circle and now was standing next to Judge Dee. While they were staring at her pale, strangely beautiful face, the judge leaned forward, quickly took the wooden hand on the table, and put it away in his sleeve. Then he rose, seized the candelabra and raised it high above his head.

They saw the huge man, who was cowering, close to the wall now, in the corner by the cabinet. His thick shoulders were hunched forward, his arms half raised, his fists clenched, as if trying to defend himself against some unseen force. His eyes were fixed on the woman's face.

Her white hand beckoned him. He righted himself and came towards her, step by step, with the jerky movements of an automaton.

The door was pushed wide open. The headman appeared, a number of constables crowded the corridor. The headman made to step inside, but the judge halted him with a peremptory gesture.

The large man kept on moving towards the woman, gazing at her face with his sunk, dull eyes as if in a trance.

'I didn't do it!' Pien shouted again. He was about to sink to the floor. Sergeant Hoong quickly supported him by his arms.

Kou and Kwang had risen too. Kou addressed the woman in black in a faltering voice:

'You must . . . How did you . . . ?'

She did not heed him. Her eyes, aglow with a strange fire, were riveted on the giant. who was now standing stock-still in front of her, his long arms pressed to his sides. Then she spoke in an even voice:

'You had plotted your scheme very well, tonight. You were waiting for me in the next street, with two horses, as we had agreed. We left the city by the south gate. You had promised to take me by a short cut to the Mandrake Grove. There I myself must gather the magic herb that would cure my sterility, and give me and my husband the long-desired son.'

She took a deep breath, then went on in the same, nearly impersonal voice:

'When we had come to the grove, you said that the herb grew inside, near the temple of the White Goddess. I was afraid crossing that dark forest, and still more afraid when you had stuck the torch between the bricks of the crumbling wall, and I saw that large marble statue. But it was you I ought to have been afraid of, Yang! Not her!'

The curio-dealer's lips moved, but she went on inexorably:

'First you brazenly spoke about your love, you said I was the most beautiful woman that ever was, you said we would go away together, nothing else mattered, only our love. When I told you aghast what I thought of you and your evil scheme, you fell on your knees, imploring me to reconsider. You wanted to kiss my feet, but I quickly stepped back, told you what you were, a treacherous lecher. Then you suddenly changed into a horrible monster.'

His towering shape seemed to shrink; he made to turn away, but he could not detach his gaze from those burning eyes. Leaning forward she said harshly:

'I accuse you here, before my dear husband, of having raped me there. You tied me naked to the marble altar, you said you would kill me slowly, cutting my veins one by one, and sprinkling my blood over the statue of the goddess. You said I would be given up as lost, no one would ever know what had happened to me. "Pray! Pray to the goddess!" you sneered. Then you left to gather more twigs for the dying torch.

'Lying there helpless on my back at the feet of the goddess, I saw above me the red ruby on her hand, glittering in the flickering light. Its red rays seemed to warm my naked body, strapped to the cold marble slab. I prayed to her, a woman herself, to help a violated woman, about to be tortured to death. I thought I felt the rope round my right wrist slacken. I tore at it in a desperate effort, and the knot slipped. I could free my hand, and I untied the other ropes. Righting myself I looked up at her in humble gratitude. In the uncertain light of the smoking torch I thought I saw her lips curve in a reassuring smile.

'Then I sprang down, wrapped my undergarment around me and slipped outside through a gap in the wall, behind the statue. I plunged into the thick undergrowth. As I struggled ahead I heard you shout for me. I went on in a blind terror, not heeding the thorns that tore my hands. Then . . .'

Suddenly she broke off. Turning half round, she gave her

158

THE WHITE GODDESS

husband a bewildered look. In a barely audible voice she added:

'No, I don't know what happened thereafter. But I have come back now, here to my own house. I . . .'

She swayed on her feet. Mr Kou hurriedly came round the table and took her arm. Looking at the judge, he stammered:

'I don't understand this at all! She didn't go out tonight, how could she have . . .'

'Your wife was speaking about what happened four years ago, Mr Kou,' Judge Dee said gravely.

XVIII

Mr Kou led her away, solicitously supporting her. The judge beckoned his men to enter. While the four constables stood themselves close by Yang, Judge Dee snapped at the headman:

'Light the wall candles!'

There was another thunderclap. Then a torrential rain came clattering down on the roof. A strong gust of wind tore at the shutters. The tempest had broken loose at last.

Dr Pien pointed at Yang.

'He . . . he gave me the powder!' he said in a tremulous voice. 'He said it was a sleeping-drug, how could I have known that it . . .'

'You stole my domino, Pien!' Judge Dee interrupted coldly.

'I can explain, explain everything, Your Honour! Yang said that he wanted Sia to go to the deserted house in Tong's place, later that night. In connection with a very important matter. Sia was to go there after the races. In the afternoon I asked Sia whether he had taken out a marker when leaving by the south gate. Sia said no. Therefore, when my eye fell on that double-blank domino, I took it and later handed it to Sia.' Giving the judge an entreating look, he wailed: 'Yang forced me to help him, sir, I swear it! I had borrowed money from him, too much money. . . . I had had such bad luck with my investments, my creditors were pressing me, my wife was harassing me, from morning till night. Yang could break my career, ruin me. . . . He gave me a small folder, told me it was a sleeping-drug, quite harmless. It looked exactly like it, I tell you! Later, when I realized I had poisoned Tong, I didn't know what to do, I . . .'

He buried his face in his hands.

'You knew the murderer, Pien!' Judge Dee said sternly. 'Your failure to denounce him makes you an accessory after the fact. The exact measure of your guilt shall be established later. Headman, let two of your men put the doctor in a palankeen and take him to jail.'

Sergeant Hoong picked up Dr Pien's stick from the floor and handed it to him. The doctor stumbled to the door, escorted by two constables.

All that time the tall curio-dealer had been standing there, still as a graven image, his broad face blank.

Now Judge Dee turned to him. Folding his arms in his sleeves he spoke:

'You abducted and raped Mrs Kou, Yang, and you shall be condemned to undergo the severest form of capital punishment, that of the lingering death. Make a full confession now, including how you had Tong Mai poisoned and the Amber Lady knifed, how you killed with your own hands Sia Kwang and Mrs Meng, and how you tried to kill your accomplice Dr Pien. If you tell the complete truth, I may propose to have the death sentence executed in a less terrible manner.'

Yang did not seem to have heard him. He was staring ahead with vacant eyes.

'You may also confess,' the judge resumed, 'that you have been robbing the temple of the White Goddess, stealing the hoard of gold the priests had stored there.'

'You'll find the golden vessels in my wall-safe,' he said in a toneless voice, 'all nine of them. Cast by one of the greatest masters of our glorious Han dynasty. I needed the money, but I couldn't bring myself to melt down those magnificent works of art. It's there, all of it. Also the ruby.' He paused. He looked hard at the judge and asked harshly: 'How did you find that out?'

'When I visited you this morning, you said that you had never been to the temple. Yet you described the altar as being separated from the pedestal. The book you showed me as source of your information states clearly that statue, pedestal and altar were carved out of one block of marble. I know, however, from a note written in the margin of my copy, that altar and pedestal were cemented together, and that the cement was removed by a later magistrate. I assumed, therefore, that you told me a lie when you said you had never visited the temple; and that, while describing the statue to me you inadvertently confused what you had read with what you had actually seen. It was only an assumption, of course; you might have read about the removal of the cement in another printed or handwritten source, unknown to me. But you confirmed it by falling into the trap I set here for you tonight.'

'So you had only vague suspicions, after all,' Yang said bitterly. 'Well, your sending the sergeant to borrow from me a white hand with a ruby ring was a clever move. It made me wonder whether you had perhaps proof of my stealing the temple hoard; or whether the hand had nothing to do with me, and was really meant only for some experiment or other. I felt that I had to know what would be discussed here tonight. I came prepared to silence you, or that coward Pien.' He pulled a long, thin knife from his bosom. The headman sprang to him, but Yang threw the knife on the table. 'Don't worry!' he sneered at the headman with a contemptuous look. Then he went on to the judge: 'I know when I am beaten. But I may as well tell you that I am an old hand in knife-throwing, and that I wouldn't have missed. But she was there . . . she was in the way.' He frowned. Suddenly he asked: 'How did you discover that it was I who nearly killed that rat Pien this afternoon?'

'I know enough about medical science,' Judge Dee replied, 'to realize that a blow on the head and a few kicks hardly justify a request not to be moved before internal injuries have been checked. One takes that precaution mainly if one has made a bad fall from a high place. Also, a footpad need not rip his victim's robe nearly in two in order to get at his money-belt. I surmised that you threw Dr Pien out of the window of your study, on the second floor. His robe caught on one of the iron spikes under the sill, and that prevented him from breaking his neck or . . .'

'I didn't throw him out of the window,' Yang interrupted gruffly. 'Pien came to see me, snivelling about the strangling of the old hag. When he said he couldn't keep silent any longer, I hit him a good blow in his face. Hadn't realized what a weak-kneed wretch he is. He crashed against the screen and tumbled out of the window before I could grab him. I rushed down and outside, and found that the spike catching his robe had broken his fall. He wasn't badly hurt, and conscious. I had to be quick, a passer-by might see us any moment. So I just told him that the little incident would have taught him a lesson, and shown him what would happen to him if ever he'd try to betray me. I said that he should pretend that he had been attacked by a robber. Then I dragged him over to the other side of the street, bleating for mercy! I could have finished him off then and there, of course. But he was owing me a lot of money, and I thought that the story of the unknown attacker would serve nicely to confuse the issue.'

Judge Dee nodded.

'Tomorrow I shall hear your full confession in the tribunal. Now I only want to check the essential points. I take it that Dr Pien spoke the truth just now about his unwittingly poisoning Tong Mai?'

'Of course! You don't think I would trust that nervous

bungler with poisoning a man, do you? I told Pien only
that I wanted Tong out of the way that night, because Sia
had to keep Tong's appointment in the old villa. I added
that I also wanted Pien's boat to lose, because I was planning to make a bit of money out of the betting. I gave Pien
the powder saying "You put this sleeping-drug in Tong's
wine-cup during the entertainment at Marble Bridge!"
Pien is afraid of me, and he owes me money, as I said before,
so he had to do as I told him. But it was no sleeping-drug,
it was a good, strong poison! I had bad luck, though. If
that confounded coroner of yours hadn't happened to be
there when Tong's body was brought on land, Pien would
have thought that the sleeping-drug had affected Tong's
heart, Tong's death would have been ascribed to heart
failure, and nobody would have been any the wiser!'

'You wanted Sia to keep Tong's rendezvous in order to
get the gold and the pearl,' Judge Dee stated curtly.

'You are wrong! I knew nothing about gold, nothing
about a pearl, I tell you! I only wanted Amber, that pre-
tentious little whore! Do you know that she refused me
when she was still a small ugly slave-maid? I told old Mr
Tong that she had tried to make up to me while I was visiting there, and I saw her get her whipping. But that wasn't
enough punishment for that lewd slut! I am sure she
bedded with Tong, even after that fool of a Kou had made
her his second lady. Tong denied it when I taxed him with
it, but he was nothing but a mean blackmailer, and she . . .
I know her sort! I would teach her, make her beg for mercy,
as did Gold Lotus there in the temple before . . . before
I . . .'

He suddenly fell silent. A sombre glow came in his eyes
as he went on softly:

'No, I should not mention that filthy little slave-maid
together with Gold Lotus. I couldn't have killed Gold Lotus

there on the altar. How could I ever have stained that perfect naked body with blood? I only wanted to cow her, in order to possess that exquisite beauty, keep it for ever, for me only. . . . One can't destroy such beauty, one can't commit such a black crime! I couldn't kill her either as she was standing here just now—four years later, yet unchanged. . . .'

He pressed his hands to his face.

There was a long pause. The only sound heard was that of the clattering rain. Kwang was surveying Yang with raised eyebrows. He wanted to say something, but the judge quickly silenced him with his raised hand. Then Yang looked up. He resumed in a detached voice:

'I had ordered Tong to repair the pavilion. The old hag's hovel wasn't safe any more. And she asked more money, and Tong asked more money—more money for those dirty, stupid women he got for me. They were dirty and stupid, but I needed them. Needed them to avenge the crime Gold Lotus had committed on me.

'I dismissed Tong, promised him a monthly allowance, to keep him quiet. I employed Sia instead, a stupid, miserable sneak thief! But I had to have someone who could keep me informed about what went on here in this house. That wretched doctor kept assuring me that Gold Lotus would never recover. But I had to check that, had to know about her, how she was living, how . . .' He paused. When he had recollected himself he went on in a steady voice: 'Sia made himself useful by worming all kinds of information out of Tong. A few days ago Sia told me that now he had definite proof that Amber slept with Tong, for they were going to have a secret meeting in the pavilion, after the races. The lecherous pair would use my couch, the couch I had placed there for strapping whores to, for my rightful revenge! But I prevented it. Sia kept Tong's appointment,

166

instead of her lover she would find there a man who would strap her to the couch she had thought she would wallow on with her lover!'

His face fell. He cursed under his breath and went on:

'Imagine the fool bungling it! When Sia came back to the city, to the house of assignation near the south gate where we had agreed to meet, the wretch was in a terrible state. He babbled about her stabbing him when he tried to strip her, and he getting panicky and killing her when trying to defend himself. To make matters worse, he had apparently been followed to the deserted house, and by officers of the tribunal! I gave him a cup of wine and told him to lie down and rest. For I needed time to think. As I made him lie down, I noticed something heavy in his sleeve. I took it out and saw that it was a package containing ten gold bars! Sia let himself roll down from the couch, he wanted to rush out of the room. But I grabbed him by his neck and put my hands round his throat. The scoundrel then confessed that he had known that Amber would be bringing that gold to the rendezvous, Sia had planned to steal it and keep it for himself. I asked Sia why she had brought all that money, and the credulous fool replied that he had heard from Tong that it was for buying from him the Emperor's pearl! Sia hadn't understood that the story of the pearl was nothing but a mean trick of Tong and his paramour to get money out of Kou for eloping together! But I didn't enlighten Sia, of course. For now that I had the gold and now that Amber had been killed, Sia would have to disappear. I told him that I would overlook his attempt at deceiving me, and even let him keep one gold bar —on condition that he help me to get the pearl. I added that he could pass the night in the house we were in, and go to the Tong villa early this morning, disguised as a carpenter.

'I went out there too, telling my assistant that I had to see a farmer about an inscribed stone he had dug up. I know a short cut to the Tong villa. Half a mile down the highway I entered the mud road next to the large farmstead there, then rode through the rice fields to the east edge of the Mandrake Grove. Three white elms mark the entrance to a narrow pathway leading through the forest to the temple, and on that same spot begins another path that circles the grove, ending up behind the Tong villa. I tethered my horse near the elm trees, then went on to the villa.

'Well, Sia did his best; he's a cunning thief, I'll say that for him! He first searched the roof of the pavilion and looked under the eaves, for Tong had told him he had hidden the pearl in a place no one would ever think of. Of course Sia found nothing there but a few bird's-nests, for the tale about the pearl had been a hoax. Then I made Sia take the interior of the pavilion apart. I thought that would give you something to think about. I have known you for more than a year, magistrate, and you are nobody's fool, I grant you that! When Sia was about through, I took up a brick and smashed his head. After I had thrown the body into the ditch, I went back to the city the same way I had come. Just before leaving I saw that smug skinflint arriving.'

Kwang began to mutter angrily, but the judge said quickly to Yang:

'I suppose you recognized Miss Lee when she was brought to the tribunal, this morning?'

'How could I've missed that silly round face?' Yang asked with disdain. 'I had told Sia that I wanted her last week. She was just the stupid type that screams her head off. When I saw her being marched to the tribunal together with three ruffians, I knew that Sia had failed to warn the men that the deal was off; that they had been caught red-handed, and would blab in the tribunal about the old hag's place. And she would promptly denounce me, of course. To save her own skin! So I rushed out there. That time I was in luck, I found her all alone!'

'Quite,' Judge Dee said dryly. 'That's all.' He gave a sign to the headman.

The judge looked on silently for a while as the constables put the giant into chains. Suddenly he spoke:

'I gather that you bore Mrs Kou and the Amber Lady a grudge because they rejected your advances. But why did you torture those other women? Women you didn't even know?'

Yang's chains rattled as he righted himself.

'I don't think you would ever understand,' he answered calmly. 'But let me try to tell you anyway. For a moment I was indeed interested in Amber because I recognized in that dirty small girl a budding beauty—as Kou did also. But Amber was nothing but empty form, inside she was just a lewd little slave-girl. As to Gold Lotus, hers is the beauty of perfect form, glowing with an inner radiance, a glow tempered by the subtle charm of breeding and refined culture. Gold Lotus represents perfect beauty: the only thing I have lived for, because it is the only thing that makes life worth living.' His voice quickened as he went on: 'Beauty as caught in stone or wood, silver or porcelain, bronze or gold can never compete with the beauty that lives and pulsates embodied in woman. And that supreme beauty must be enjoyed by physical possession, every day to be admired and gazed at, stroked and fondled, ever revealing new charms, new delights. Possessing Gold Lotus was the ultimate goal of my life, the crowning delight that my long years of loving, preserving, and studying beauty had fully entitled me to. That night, in the temple, she murdered me. With one cruel blow she killed my capacity for enjoying beauty, leaving me maimed, with nothing but the desire for revenge.

With the burning desire to avenge the cruel, inhuman crime committed against me!' His eyes glittered with a maniacal gleam as he exclaimed exulting: 'I have taken that revenge! I, a murdered man risen from the grave! I have tortured woman, the heartless murderess, she who tempts and entices man with coy smiles and shy glances, then to repel him with a sneer, leaving him a pitiable wreck, crippled in both body and mind. All those others I made grovel before me begged for mercy in her voice, it was her flesh I lacerated, her blood I saw flow, her . . .' He broke off and licked the foam from his snarling lips. Suddenly his distorted face relaxed. He said quietly: 'I did what I felt I had to do. I shall take the consequences.'

Judge Dee nodded at the headman. Yang was led away.

The judge sat down. He wiped the perspiration from his forehead. Mr Kwang cleared his throat and asked:

'Would Your Honour kindly allow me to ask a question?' As Judge Dee nodded wearily, he went on: 'Mr Yang owes me a not inconsiderable sum for two antique bronzes supplied to him. Am I correct in assuming that the tribunal will in due time pay out that amount to me from the dead criminal's confiscated assets?'

'Indeed, Mr Kwang,' Judge Dee replied. Then he added: 'I need you tomorrow in the tribunal, as a witness. Thereafter you are free to continue your journey, any time you like.'

'Thank you, sir.' Sadly shaking his head, Kwang went on: 'I had always considered both Mr Yang and Dr Pien sound businessmen! Goes to show one can't be too careful in choosing the persons to deal with! I am most grateful that Your Honour allowed me to take part in tonight's session, it was a very instructive experience. I take it that you knew beforehand that Yang and Pien were guilty, sir?'

'I did,' Judge Dee replied in order to get rid of him.

'Wonderful! Would you believe, sir, that I actually
had a fleeting impression that you were suspecting me too?
Tsk tsk, how little do we ignorant merchants understand
the subtleties of the official mind!'

'You may go now, Mr Kwang,' the judge said sourly.
'Convey my best wishes to Mr Sun.'

'Thank you, sir. Mr Sun will certainly appreciate that.'
He pursed his lips and went on worriedly: 'Mr Sun is in
for another attack, I fear. I am familiar with the symptoms.
When, directly after the noon meal today, he started to
belch and complained of . . .'

'Will you kindly see Mr Kwang out, Hoong?' Judge
Dee interrupted.

Kwang made a low bow. The sergeant conducted him to
the corridor.

'Preposterous fellow!' Judge Dee muttered disgustedly.
He groped in his sleeve and brought out the wooden hand.
He carefully detached it from the back of the small tortoise
it had been glued to. The animal remained motionless on
the table, its head and limbs securely drawn in.

Sergeant Hoong came back. He silently went to the corner-
table, felt whether the teapot was still warm, then poured
out a cup.

'Give our friend here the leaves you were holding up
behind my three guests, Hoong!'

The sergeant came up to the table and set the cup down
in front of the judge. Then he took a bunch of green leaves
from his sleeve. As soon as he had put them on the table,
the tortoise stuck its head out, blinked at the candle, then
eagerly crawled to the leaves.

XIX

Sergeant Hoong looked on in silence while Judge Dee was slowly emptying his cup. There was a hurt look on his old, wrinkled face. When the judge had finished, Hoong said dejectedly:

'This afternoon Your Honour told me all about the trap set for Kou, Pien and Kwang. You didn't say one word about Yang, sir.'

'Take a seat Hoong,' the judge said quietly. He loosened the front of his robe and pushed his cap back from his brow. Resting his forearms on the table, he began:

'The clue of the missing domino suggested that the number of suspects must be limited to Kou, Pien and Kwang. That one of these three had been acting on the orders of a fourth person was a remote possibility. A possibility I kept in mind only because of a vague, intuitive feeling that the manner of the last two murders was wrong. Sia and Mrs Meng were killed in a violent, savage manner. I couldn't help thinking that Kou, Pien or Kwang would have stabbed Sia from behind rather than brutally smash his head, and that they would have put poison in Mrs Meng's tea rather than viciously strangling her. Further, the murders took place in quick succession and in widely separated places, suggesting a powerful, very active man, accustomed to strenuous rides up and down the country-side. Neither Kou nor Pien fitted that description, nor Kwang; that exasperating businessman does travel about a lot, but always in a comfortable junk.

'Since the murderer had to be connected with the antique trade, I thought of course of Yang, as a fourth suspect.

172

Physically he fitted my intuitive picture of the criminal, and he had the same opportunities for committing the crimes as Kou, Pien or Kwang. Yang was present at the boat race and showed special interest in our diagnosis of Tong's death; this morning he had gone out for a ride up-country, so he could have killed Sia; and he was in the neighbourhood of the tribunal when Miss Liang went there to report the prostitute's abduction. Further, there were three points against him. First, although he assured me he had never visited the ruined temple, he knew about the altar being separated from the statue's pedestal. This suggested that he had indeed visited the temple, probably in order to rob it. Second, his pretending not to know Tong and Sia, which seemed highly improbable since those two were engaged in the same trade. Third, his contradicting Sheng Pa's information that Dr Pien needed money; this suggested that Pien was Yang's henchman, whom he wanted to protect against all possible suspicion.'

The judge waited till Sergeant Hoong had refilled his cup, then went on:

'However, every one of these three points had a perfectly innocent alternative. Yang might have read in some other antiquarian treatise about the change made in the temple. Tong and Sia might have deliberately avoided Yang as a dangerous competitor in the curio trade. And Dr Pien might have concealed his financial difficulty so well that only Sheng Pa's all-seeing and all-hearing beggars could come to know about it. And, most important of all: Yang had no motive. I knew Yang and his habits fairly well; if there was a motive, I thought that its roots must lie somewhere in the past. But there was no time for a detailed investigation, I had to take immediate measures. And measures that would allow me to check my logical deductions as well as my vague intuition.

173

'Thus I laid tonight's trap, intended for all four suspects, all at the same time. If Kou, Pien or Kwang were the criminal, I hoped that my reading out of the faked letter, my dark hints about the criminal having made a mistake, my macabre talk about avenging ghosts culminating in the sudden appearance of the white hand, would frighten the guilty person into betraying himself—as I explained to you in detail before we came here. What I did not tell you then was that I expected Yang, if he were indeed the criminal, to come here to spy on us.

'Before we left the tribunal, you heard me tell the head-man to follow us here and, as soon as I had sent Kou's steward away, to round up all the servants except the gate-keeper, and herd them together in a back room. Then he and his men were to hide themselves beyond the bend of the corridor. They were to arrest anyone who should leave the library, but they were not to interfere with anybody coming from outside. These instructions were meant to make sure that Kou, Pien or Kwang would not escape if one of them were the criminal and, at the same time, to facilitate Yang's spying on us—if *he* were our man. Well, my intuition proved to be right. Yang was the murderer and he fell into my trap. You yourself heard him state just now that he had indeed come prepared to take action—which would have proved beyond doubt that he was the criminal.'

'You took a terrible risk, sir! If I had known that, I would never have agreed to the plan. Never!'

Judge Dee gave his old assistant an affectionate look. He said soberly:

'Now you know the reason why I didn't tell you about that particular part of my scheme, Hoong.'

'You were right, sir! I was terribly afraid as it was! As the tension kept mounting, I expected every moment one of those three men to attack you!'

174

'I didn't feel too well myself!' Judge Dee said with a wan smile. 'I had seen this room only once before and mistakenly assumed that, when the candelabras along the back wall were out, the large candle on the table here would allow me to watch the door on my right and the three men opposite me, all at once. If Yang comes to spy on us, I thought, I'll notice his setting the door ajar, and if he should rush inside later to attack me or his accomplice, I'll have plenty of time to tackle him and shout for the constables. As it was, however, I could see on my right only black shadows, and I found it impossible to deliver my speech, and yet keep an eye on the door as well as on my three suspects all the time. When I knew that someone was inside, and heard the sound of breathing close behind me, I was struck by the uncomfortable thought that this time I had tempted providence too far!'

He passed his hand over his eyes, then went on in a tired voice:

'Now that I have heard Yang's confession, I understand that it all began with his love for Gold Lotus. This infatuation became tangled with his passionate love of fine art, the two finally blending into the frenzied desire of a lonely elderly man to possess and enjoy what he soon was to lose forever. Possessing Gold Lotus in the ruined temple, yet irrevocably losing her, incapacitated him in mind and body, and engendered in him a maniacal rage, which he sought to appease vicariously by maltreating other women.' He heaved a sigh, then resumed: 'As to Pien, according to the law he should be beheaded. But since there are mitigating circumstances for the misguided doctor, I shall propose to have his death sentence commuted to a long prison term. Remind me, Hoong, to make arrangements for Miss Lee, after the case has been disposed of. We'll give her a round sum from the confiscated assets of Yang, so that her father can redeem

175

her. She impressed me as a staunch girl, she deserves better than life in a brothel.'

For a while Judge Dee watched the tortoise that was nibbling contentedly at the green leaves. Then he spoke:

'This small animal did his duty, Hoong. But things turned out quite differently from what I had thought. Now it is clear what actually happened, of course. When I ordered our headman to round up all the servants in this house, I had completely forgotten about Mrs Kou. Our good headman has a one-track mind, he collared also the maids assigned to look after that poor lady. Left alone in her room, she went out and started to wander about in the empty house. She must have seen Yang going to this room, but he didn't see her. Yang had avoided meeting her ever since his raping her in the ruined temple. He told me he had made it a point never to go farther than the reception room when visiting here, allegedly because he couldn't bear to see Kou's beautiful collection. The real reason was of course that he didn't dare to risk meeting Gold Lotus, who might recognize him and remember. Tonight she did not, at first, recognize Yang, but the mere seeing of him must have stirred something in her deranged mind, and she followed him to the library here. You saw her come inside, Hoong. She passed by Yang, who was standing in the corner to the left of the door, went on towards the light circle and stood herself behind my chair. Now it so happened that tonight a storm was threatening, it was exactly the same tense and oppressive atmosphere as on that night four years ago, when Yang abducted her. Mentally deranged persons are especially sensitive to weather conditions, and the similar atmosphere prepared the way for what followed. When I put the white hand with the red ruby on the table, she saw the marble hand of the goddess, the hand she had looked up to in that terrible moment when she was lying helpless on the altar. Suddenly she connected

176

the hand with the man she had just seen, and in a flash everything came back. She was cured by the shock.'

Sergeant Hoong nodded.

'Heaven has been kind to Mr Kou,' he remarked. 'In its mercy it took the adulterous Amber Lady away, and restored his faithful wife to him, completely cured.' He frowned, then asked curiously: 'How did Your Honour know that, on the night that Yang abducted Mrs Kou, a storm was threatening? I don't remember her mentioning that.'

'Nobody mentioned it. But don't you see that the ghostly apparition of the White Lady that four years ago frightened the Tong family so much was in fact Mrs Kou? Her mind distracted by the terrible experience in the temple, she must somehow or other have found her way to the edge of the grove. Everything fits! She was half naked, her hair was hanging loose, and the thorny branches had torn her hands and limbs, hence the blood the Tong family saw. Then the tempest started, and the poor deranged woman walked round the grove and wandered the rest of the night through the fields, till she collapsed from sheer exhaustion outside the east gate, where the next morning the farmers found her. I'll check the precise dates, of course, but I don't doubt for one moment that the abduction of Gold Lotus and the ghostly phenomenon in the Tong villa will prove to have occurred on one and the same night!'

Alone in the large room, the two men sat listening silently to the rain. At last Sergeant Hoong spoke up with a satisfied smile:

'So Your Honour has solved two baffling puzzles tonight! One concerning no less than four murders, and also that old riddle of the White Goddess.'

Judge Dee took a sip from his tea. After he had set his cup down he gave the sergeant a thoughtful look and said slowly:

'The murders, yes, I solved those. And also that one appearance of the goddess, four years ago.' Shaking his head he went on: 'As to her part in all that happened here . . . no, I haven't solved that, Hoong.' He got up from his chair and replaced the small tortoise in his sleeve. Straightening his robe he said: 'It seems the rain has abated a little. Let's go back to the tribunal.'

XX

The following morning, shortly after dawn, Judge Dee and Sergeant Hoong left the city by the south gate and rode out into the country. The storm of the preceding night had cleared the air, and it promised to become a beautiful, cool day.

The judge had sat up till deep in the night, drawing up a full report on the murders, to be forwarded to the higher authorities. He had slept badly. He had found it difficult to ban the tense moments in Kou's library from his mind, and he did not relish the prospect of hearing Yang's confession all over again, during the morning session of the tribunal.

Having risen after a fitful slumber, he had decided to make an early trip with Hoong to the Mandrake Grove in order to survey the possibility of having the forest cleared. He planned to append a proposal to that effect to his report on the murders, pointing out that the continued existence of such a place would tempt miscreants to make their lair there.

They took the short cut through the rice fields indicated by the curio-dealer. Soon the tall trees of the forest came into sight.

They easily located the white elm trees that marked the pathway leading to the ruined temple. However, they found that the tempest had played havoc there; uprooted trees had fallen across the path amidst a tangle of thick creepers and thorny shrubs, effectively barring their progress.

The two men circled the grove, looking all the time for other gaps. But they found nothing but an impenetrable wall of old trees and thick undergrowth.

At last they found themselves at the back of the deserted house. They rode along its outer wall, to the entrance. Judge Dee dismounted there. He said to the sergeant:

'Let's have a look at the grove from the walled-in garden. Four years ago Mrs Kou emerged somewhere there from among the trees. It is our last chance of finding a way to get inside!'

They passed through the tunnel-like entrance, and went to the side garden to the east of the main building.

Standing at the low wall, they scanned the forbidding mass of trees. No leaf stirred in the still morning air. Twittering birds flew in and out from under the eaves of the pavilion, but they shunned the forest. There everything was as quiet as the grave. A strange air of silent expectancy seemed to linger among the dark foliage.

After a long time Judge Dee shook his head. He spoke:

'No, I shan't disturb the abode of the White Goddess, after all. We shall leave her in peace, standing there in her ruined temple, in the middle of her sacred grove. There are things, Hoong, that are better let well alone. Let's go back to the city!'

As he turned round, his eye fell on a young bird that was struggling helplessly among the grass, near the wall of the pavilion. It frantically flapped its undeveloped, naked wings. Judge Dee carefully took it up in his cupped hands and said:

'Poor fellow fell out of its nest! It doesn't seem to have hurt itself, though.' Lifting his head he went on: 'Look, the nest is up there under the eaves of the pavilion, the mother is flying around it. I'll put it back.'

He climbed on the low wall and put the bird in the nest. But instead of stepping down he remained standing there. Raising himself on tiptoe, he had a close look, not heeding the mother bird that flapped anxiously round his head.

Amidst broken egg-shells three young birds were huddling close together, squeaking with wide open beaks. By their side lay an egg-shaped object. The dirt clinging to it could not conceal its shining white colour.

Judge Dee took it up with his thumb and forefinger, then stepped down. He rubbed it clean with his handkerchief. Having laid it in the palm of his left hand, he silently examined it, Sergeant Hoong looking on. It sent forth a purely white, shimmering brilliance. After a while Judge Dee said softly:

'This is the Emperor's Pearl, Hoong!'

The sergeant sucked in his breath. Bending over Judge Dee's hand he stared at the pearl. Then he asked, involuntarily lowering his voice:

'Couldn't it be a fake, sir?'

The judge shook his head.

'No, Hoong. No one could ever imitate that perfect shape, and that unearthly white shine. Tong Mai's story was true, this is indeed the long-lost Imperial treasure. Tong was a resourceful crook, he had indeed hidden the pearl in the pavilion, but in a place where no one would discover it. When Sia searched the eaves he saw the nest, but then the eggs had not yet hatched, apparently. And we would never have found it but for this lucky chance—if it was a chance.' Letting the shining pearl move slowly in his palm, he resumed with a sigh: 'So, after all these long years, after untold human suffering, and after the shedding of so much innocent blood, this pearl shall revert to the Throne, its rightful owner.'

He reverently wrapped the pearl up in his handkerchief and put it in his bosom. Then he resumed:

'I shall hand the pearl to Mr Kou, together with an official statement signed by me saying that a murder-case prevented Kou from reporting at once that he had news

181

about the discovery of the lost treasure. Thus Mr Kou shall travel to the capital without any misgivings, and present the pearl to the Palace. I hope that the honours the Emperor will bestow upon him, together with the recovery of Gold Lotus, will reconcile him to the loss of the Amber Lady.

'As to her, I did her a grievous injustice, Hoong. She never had an affair with Tong Mai, and she had not planned to elope with him. She only wanted to acquire this rare treasure for Mr Kou, as a mark of her gratitude to the man who had reshaped her life, elevated her from her wretched condition to become his Second Lady, and whose child she was bearing. Tong Mai she knew only as the son of her former master, who occasionally purchased curios for her husband. She knew nothing of his foul dealings with Yang. My theory about that aspect of the case was completely wrong. I made a very big mistake, and I can do nothing to correct it. The only thing I can do is to apologize humbly to her departed soul.'

The judge stood there silently for a while, his eyes on the dark foliage of the Mandrake Grove, beyond the low garden wall. Then he turned round abruptly and motioned Sergeant Hoong to follow him. They walked back to the gatehouse, mounted their horses, and rode to Marble Bridge Village.

In the market-place the vendors were busy setting up their stalls. There were no other people about at this early hour.

A thin morning haze was hanging over the placid brown water of the Canal, its shreds drifted among the trees overshadowing the small shrine of the River Goddess on the waterside. The old priest was sweeping the fallen leaves from the steps with a long bamboo broom.

The old man looked up indifferently as Judge Dee dismounted and went up the steps. Obviously he did not recognize him as the magistrate.

182

Blue clouds curled up from the incense burner on the altar, filling the shrine with a subtle fragrance. Through the clouds the judge could vaguely see the face of the goddess, her lips curved in a faint smile.

Standing there with his arms folded in his wide sleeves and looking up at the still face, he let the events of the last two days pass before his mind's eye. There had been strange coincidences. But did there really exist such a thing as a coincidence? How little did he really know about the minds and motives of his fellow-men! Could he ever dare then to try to understand the powers on high that disposed their destinies?

He said, softly:

'You are only a man-made idol, but you stand as a symbol of what man cannot know, and is not destined to know. As such, I make my humble bow to you.'

When he had righted himself and turned to go he found the old priest standing behind him. He felt in his sleeve for a few coppers. Suddenly his fingers closed round a silver piece. He took it out and regarded it for a while, deep in sombre thought. It was the same silver piece the Amber Lady had given to him.

He handed it to the priest and said:

'On the fifth of every month you shall burn a stick of incense here, and offer a prayer for the rest of the soul of Mrs Kou, personal name Amber.'

The old man accepted the silver with a respectful bow. He went to the side-table and opened the bulky register lying there. After he had wetted the worn-down writing brush, he laboriously entered the donation in the book, his grey head bent close to the yellowish page.

Judge Dee went out and descended the stairs. He took the reins from Sergeant Hoong and swung himself on his horse.

Suddenly the old priest appeared at the head of the steps, still holding the writing brush in his wrinkled hand. He asked in a quavering voice:

'What name shall I enter for the donor, revered sir? And what is the gentleman's honourable profession?'

Turning round in the saddle the judge replied shortly:

'Just write: Dee from Tai-yuan.' Then he added with a rueful sigh: 'A student.'

POSTSCRIPT

JUDGE DEE was a historical person, a famous statesman of the Tang dynasty, who lived from 630 to 700 A.D. During the first half of his career, when he was serving as magistrate in various districts, he solved a great many mysterious crimes. Even today, therefore, Judge Dee is remembered by the Chinese people as their master-detective, his name being as familiar to them as Sherlock Holmes is to us. The adventures related here, however, are entirely fictitious.

Note that in Judge Dee's time the Chinese did not wear pigtails; that custom was imposed on them after 1644 A.D., when the Manchus had conquered China. The men did their hair up in a top-knot, and wore caps both inside and outside the house. They did not smoke; tobacco and opium were introduced into China only many centuries later.

30-vi-1962   Robert van Gulik